I0680295

Fowl Campaign

SILVER HILLS COZY MYSTERIES, Volume 8

Sam Cheever

Published by Electric Prose Publications, 2019.

FOWL CAMPAIGN

First edition. April 5, 2019.

Written by Sam Cheever.

***COME TO SILVER HILLS.** Where fowl plans can either mean dinner out, or the deadly designs of a chicken-livered killer.*

When Vlad's opponent for the Silver City mayoral race succumbs to fowl deeds, he seriously changes the pecking order in Vlad's favor. But the victim's death has made Vlad king of the roost, so the Silver Hills night manager quickly becomes the obvious suspect.

Plucky investigators Flo and Co. are certainly no strangers to Vlad's evil ways. But they're also not egg-xactly convinced he did it. So, when Flo learns that the victim, a wealthy local chicken farmer, had been trying to reach her when he was killed, she's more than a little curious why.

Will their investigation shine a light on a killer's fowl deeds before he flies the coop? Or will Flo chicken out when the villain threatens to go all cock-a-doodle-do on her bad self? There's only one way to find out. And you already know what it is...

Yep, Flo and Co. are goin' in, tail feathers high!

Sam doesn't give away a lot of books. But she values her readers and, to show it, she's gifting you a copy of a fun book just for signing up for her newsletter!
<u>SIGN UP HERE!</u>[1]

SAM CHEEVER

https://samcheever.com/newsletter/

CHAPTER ONE

FLO, AGNES, AND CELIA stood on the sidewalk with their mouths hanging open. The big bus lumbered noisily by, its side befouled by a giant banner that said, *Vote for Vlad*, with a picture of the Silver Hills night manager's hated face.

"Why is he orange?" Agnes asked, frowning.

"They must have used spray tan to take away that undead look," Flo speculated. She shook her head as the monstrosity wound its way down Main Street and turned at the next light. "It's like we're living in an alternate universe."

Celia nodded. "I saw one of his campaign commercials this morning." She turned her frown to Flo. "It said he was Woke. What does that even mean?"

"It means his writers have poor English," Flo mused.

"Maybe it's a Vamp thing," Agnes added. "You know, beware villagers, the vampire is woke. Grab the pitchforks."

"I'm pretty sure that isn't what it means, Agnes," Celia said with a smile.

"I know one thing, I was woke too early this morning," Agnes grumbled. "I'm tired."

"The trash truck?" Flo asked. Unfortunately for Agnes, the dumpsters for the residence were right outside her window and every Tuesday they woke her up at five AM. Her friend definitely looked tired. She had purple arcs beneath her expressive gray eyes and her graying brown pageboy hairstyle was rumpled looking, as if she'd done a lot of tossing and turning.

Flo resisted the urge to smooth her own, freshly dyed blonde bouff as she gave Agnes a sympathetic look. She had shadows under her hazel eyes too. Flo's circles were from lying awake worrying about the rift between her and her friend TC.

"I'd complain again to Richard but it won't do any good," Agnes murmured.

"You're the weekend manager," Celia said quite reasonably. "Can't you make a new rule or something? Maybe request a schedule change?"

"I've tried. But Tuesday's aren't my days and Richard insists he's tried to move the time. They aren't budging."

"I think I'd be tempted to move to another apartment," Celia said. "I need my beauty sleep."

"Me too!" Agnes lamented, running her hands through the air in front of her six-foot-tall, widely-made form. "You don't think all this beauty comes easy, do you?"

Celia chuckled.

"Easily," Flo corrected. "Oh, look."

They all turned their focus across the street, where an attractive, dark-haired young woman was standing with her back to them, pretending to read a flyer that was taped to the window. She was clearly observing them in the reflection of the glass at *Cooper's Beauty Products*.

"She's watching us again," Agnes said on a frown. "It's kind of creepy."

Flo felt like crying. "TC's not creepy, Agnes. She's just struggling." Flo waved and TC ducked her head, hurrying on down the street as if she hadn't seen them.

"It's her own fault," Celia said in her customary hardline way. "She's the one keeping herself away."

"Maybe she needs to be Woke," Agnes observed, pursing her lips.

Flo started off down the street. "*Woke* my narrow behind. That's just a misuse of the language if you ask me."

"I think it means you like transvestites."

Celia and Flo stopped in their tracks and looked at Agnes in shock. "Why in the world would Vlad have a campaign commercial saying he likes transvestites?"

Agnes shrugged. "Who knows. Maybe Dave Potts is really a woman."

Potts was running against Vlad for the position of Mayor of Silver City. Since he went about three hundred pounds and had more hair on his face than most men had on their entire bodies, it seemed unlikely he was actually a woman.

"You're being ridiculous," Flo told her friend.

"I think it means you like gays," Celia offered.

"Potts could be gay," Agnes offered as they stepped off the curb and crossed the street to the Silver Hills Senior and Singles Residence.

"Even if he is," Flo countered. "Why would Vlad proclaim he liked him in a campaign commercial?"

"To grab the gay constituency, of course." Agnes said. Then she frowned. "I didn't mean that like it sounded. Though I guess Vlad could be gay too. His great, great, great ancestor was kind of Metro Sexual-ish if you ask me."

Celia, having less experience with Agnes' contorted thought processes, frowned. "Metro Sexuals aren't gay, Agnes. Well, not completely."

Flo sighed. "She's talking about Dracula."

"Ah." Celia grinned. "Vlad does kind of look like Count Dracula."

"The cereal or the actor?" Agnes asked with a grin.

Agnes and Celia shared a laugh as Flo reached for the front doors. "You two are impossible. Now, we need to sit down and figure out how to get TC back into the fold. She's breaking my heart."

Agnes veered left as soon as they came through the door, heading for the dining area, which was starting to fill up for happy hour. Several people hailed her as she strode quickly toward the big, round tables and Agnes stopped to shake hands and say a few words at every table she passed.

Celia bumped Flo's arm and chuckled. "If I didn't know better, I'd think Agnes was the one running for Mayor."

Flo's eyes widened. "Good Heavens. Don't even say such a thing in jest. Can you imagine? Her slogan would be, a pie on every table, a Twinkie in every drawer."

Celia laughed, wrapping her arm around Flo's shoulders. "Sounds good to me."

Flo had to admit to herself that Agnes would be a much better mayor than either of the people currently throwing their hat in the ring for the job.

Dave Potts was a thoroughly unlikeable fellow. He was brash and aggressive, and seemed not to care much about anything except his own rise to power and wealth. His family had a large chicken farm outside of Silver Hills, the stench of which permeated the air all through town if the wind was blowing wrong. Potts Chickens were sold across the country and he'd built up quite a business. But he'd apparently grown bored with being a Chicken King and had decided he could rule Silver City too.

Flo personally thought his crown might be a little too tight. He was so unlikeable there was little chance anybody would seriously consider him for the job. Although, given his competition, there might be a lot of nose holding happening on election day. And it wouldn't be caused by the stench of chicken poop.

Nothing needed to be said about Vladwick Newsome. A more reprehensible human being would be difficult to find. Unless one cast her gaze toward Potts.

Choosing between the two men would be a soul-crushing, psyche-scarring event that Flo was not looking forward to. She was still hoping a third candidate would surface, giving them a real choice for mayor.

"Let's go," Celia murmured in an urgent tone. "Here comes Elisa. She's heading right for us."

Elisa Kemp was Silver Hills' self-proclaimed queen of all knowledge. She knew everything about everybody and if she didn't know something, she knew how to get the information. Flo had found the woman's busy-body network handy a time or two when trying to solve a crime, but as a social acquaintance, Elisa was a bit hard to take.

Flo never knew when Elisa's rumor-fed mind was targeting *her* life for future information sharing. It was an occupational hazard for Flo since she'd decided to become a private investi-gator of sorts. One that she knew she had to embrace, no matter what it cost. She flicked her fingers toward Agnes, across the room. "You go on, Ce. I'll talk to Elisa and see what she wants. Maybe she's heard something about a new candidate for mayor." *Hope springs eternal*, Flo mused to herself.

Celia patted her on the back and hurried away, anxious to avoid the sour, snoopy Elisa.

Flo smiled as the woman hurried up to her, her trademark hangdog expression plastered across her narrow face. She reached cold, bony fingers to Flo, clasping her hands quickly before dropping them. "I have news about the mayoral race."

Flo let her excitement show in her expression, feeding the other woman's ego. "Please tell me there's going to be a third candidate."

Elisa blinked, her gaze tightening with pique. "How would I know that, Flo?"

How did the woman know anything? Flo asked herself. "Oh, I'm sorry, I thought when you said you had news..."

Elisa pursed her thin lips, flapping her hands in the air between them. As always, she reminded Flo of an enormous praying mantis with pincers for lips. "Flo, listen to me. This is important."

Flo's mouth slammed shut and she clasped her hands in front of her, giving Elisa her patient teacher look.

The other woman's hand swept over a loose, gray-black strand of hair on her temple, smoothing it back into the over-tight bun at the nape of her long neck.

She hunched her Ichabod Crane-like form and lowered her head toward Flo, her breath tinged with garlic from her lunch of spaghetti and meatballs. "Dave Potts needs to see you."

Flo blinked "Really? Why? I barely know the man." Flo was pretty sure she'd taught Potts's sons a decade earlier, when she'd worked as a substitute school teacher. She'd met his wife a few times but couldn't recall having met the candidate face to face, except maybe in passing at a school event.

Elisa shrugged bony shoulders. "I have no idea. I got word through my grapevine that he's trying to contact you. Apparently, he's called here a few times and Vlad's hung up on him."

Flo frowned. "I hope he's not looking for dirt on Vlad. I don't like the man, but I'm not going to insert myself into this race. The two men will need to sink or swim without me."

But Elisa was shaking her head. The errant strand of hair flew from the bun again, yearning to be free. "I don't think that's it. Beatrice Barker overheard Vlad demanding to know what Potts wanted with you. She inferred from Vlad's side of the conversation that Potts wouldn't tell him."

"Oh my!" Flo breathed out. Then it hit her. "Potts wants to hire me as an investigator?"

"It seems that way, yes." Elisa's expression turned sly. "Is there any kind of—erm—finder's fee or anything?"

Flo barely kept from rolling her eyes. "Don't get ahead of yourself, Elisa. Let me talk to the man. If he ends up hiring me I'll cut you in for a small fee." Though it sounded as if she should be paying the fee to Beatrice Barker instead.

Elisa's pincer lips tightened. "How small?"

"We'll discuss it later." Flo started to turn away and then realized she needed to keep Elisa in her corner. She bit back a sigh, turning to offer the other woman a tight smile. "Thanks for bringing this to me, Elisa."

Elisa nodded. "You'll keep me informed?"

"Absolutely. Bye now."

Flo hurried toward the group surrounding Agnes at their usual table. It was a lively group, filled with several of the younger residents from the singles side of the building. But Flo wasn't interested in joining the throng. She was making a bee-line toward Bea Barker.

CHAPTER TWO

"I HONESTLY DON'T KNOW why Potts was trying to get hold of you," Bea insisted. "Vlad did deny sending somebody to Potts. I have no idea what that meant." She shifted in her chair, sending a cloud of sweet-smelling white powder into the air around her. The table around Bea's place setting was dusted with the stuff, and the chair back Flo was resting her hands on was slippery with it.

Beatrice was addicted to talcum powder. She dusted herself with it several times a day. The result was that the woman resembled a talcum powder Pigpen, like from the Charlie Brown cartoons. Clouds of the stuff misted into the air every time she moved. She shook her head and a fine spray of dust drifted away, finding Flo's nose and making her sneeze.

"Oh my goodness, Flo," Bea said with a concerned frown. "I hope you aren't coming down with something."

Flo sniffed. "Nothing that won't be cured with a little time and distance."

Bea's brow furrowed more deeply. "Oh. Um, well, as I already told you, I walked into the office to make my phone payment and Vlad was standing by Morticia's desk, the phone at his ear. His fangs were dripping with venom over whatever he was hearing on the other end. He cast the evil eye on me, of course, but I persevered. I stood there until he slammed the phone down on the desk."

"You heard him say Dave Potts's name?"

"Not really. What he actually said was that he wasn't—and I quote—that horrible woman's secretary, and if she wanted to start her own business and take on chicken-livered reprobates as clients, it was no skin off his nose."

"So that's what you're basing the assumption on that it was Dave Potts?"

Bea scratched her Geisha-girl-colored face and powder rose up in a fog around her finger. "That, and the fact that, before Vlad slammed the phone down, he said, 'Go play with your chickens. You're going to need to keep that job because you're not going to get a new one anytime soon.'"

Flo sighed wearily. "You might have led with that, Bea."

Bea's grin was slow and slightly dusty. "Might I have?"

"I'M NOT KIDDING, FLO, this is bringing back too many unsettling memories."

A biting menthol smell stung Flo's nostrils. She looked around for the source, seeing nothing. "I don't think Dave Potts has pigs, Agnes. Besides, if you don't stick your hand blindly through any fences, you should be fine."

Sitting in the passenger seat of Flo's car, Agnes shuddered violently. "I'll never forget the feeling of that monster's teeth on my hand."

Flo rolled her eyes. "That *monster* is very sweet. I'm pretty sure he only licked you. There were no teeth involved." Agnes was referring to Rufus, the inquisitive and overly friendly porcine pet of a local man who lived outside Silver City, not too far from where they were currently driving.

"Chickens are more my cup of tea," Agnes proclaimed.

Flo scanned her a glance. "Have you ever met a chicken?"

"Well, not a live one. But they taste really good fried and in chicken salad with grapes and walnuts."

Flo shook her head. "I've heard chickens can be nasty and dirty."

Her friend shrugged. "At least they don't have teeth."

Flo didn't bother reminding her friend that they did have beaks and claws. She figured Agnes was going to do what Agnes was going to do. The only thing Flo could hope to accomplish was, maybe, keeping her friend from falling into a plucking machine or something with equal maiming potential.

Menthol wafted past Flo again and she looked down at her clothes, wondering what she could have spilled on them. Had she worn the same tee-shirt when she had chest congestion a few weeks earlier? There had to be something in the car. She'd search under the seats when they got home.

Flo slowed for the turn into Potts Farms. Fortunately, the actual chicken production part of the setup was in the distance, though the smell certainly traveled.

She frowned at the slide of orange colored paper across the gravel and grass of the entrance. It looked like someone had dumped a trash can on the road. Except all of the trash was the same. She recognized the flyer TC had been perusing in Silver

City and made a mental note to take a closer look when she got a chance.

Clearly, something was in the works. Though the flyers were probably of the political variety. Campaign flyers. She thought she'd seen a chicken on the front of one as it blew past.

As Flo pulled up to the big ranch house and climbed out of her car, she had to cover her face with one hand to mask the stench. "Oh my!"

Agnes lumbered around the car, her gaze locked onto the big, stone house. "Looks like Potts is doing okay for himself."

Flo couldn't disagree. She figured she was looking at a million dollar home on what was probably close to three hundred acres. But the ambiance could certainly use some help. "Let's get this over with. If I take him on as a client, I'mb insisting on meeting him in tdown next tdime."

Agnes threw her a look. "Are you getting a cold? You sound all nasally."

"Imb breathing through mby mouth. Don't you smelb that?"

Agnes shrugged. "I don't smell anything."

Flo hurried toward the front door and knocked, wondering if she'd have to breathe through her nose to speak with Potts when he answered the door.

She wasn't going to get an answer to that, because Potts didn't answer the door.

"I guess we need to go over there and look for him," Agnes said, pointing toward the distant building.

Flo shuddered at the thought. If it smelled that bad where they were, it was probably going to send her to her knees when she got closer.

"Can I help you?"

Flo jerked around in surprise. A woman was coming around the side of the house, gardening gloves in one hand and a basket filled with cut flowers in the other. She squinted against the sun behind Flo and tipped her head to one side. "Florence Bee?"

Flo finally recognized her. Hurrying forward, she gave Nanna Potts a smile. "Mrs. Potts. How are you?"

"Call me Nanna, please. What a nice surprise." The woman settled her basket of flowers onto the ground and draped the well-worn gloves over the handle. "I haven't seen you in years."

Flo nodded, the memory of their last meeting coming back to her. "The Spring Fling dance. I remember." As a substitute teacher for the Silver City school system, Flo had volunteered to chaperone one of the eighth-grade dances. She'd spent the evening chatting with Nanna Potts and had found her to be a kind, warm person who'd worried about her sons' awkwardness and poor social skills just as any mother would. "How are the boys?"

Nanna's smile was wide, proud. "David's working in Indy these days. He's got an important position with a financial planning company. Pet's at Indiana University School of Medicine, studying to be a doctor."

If Flo remembered correctly, Pet was short for Peter. It had apparently been a family nickname that had stuck. "That's wonderful. You must be so proud."

"I am, of course. The boys always did have more brains than social skills." She laughed easily.

"I'm sure they do just fine with the girls. I recall that they were quite handsome." It was only a small lie. David Junior had been a pudgy child with rosy cheeks and a messy cap of dark brown hair that always seemed to stick up in weird places. Peter had been slender, like his mother, but acne had plagued him throughout middle school and Flo wondered if he'd gotten a handle on it.

"They have a lot of friends," Nanna responded. "So, what brings you out here?"

Agnes cleared her throat and Flo realized she hadn't introduced the two women. "My manners are atrocious. I'm so sorry." She grabbed Agnes's arm and tugged her forward. "This is my friend, Agnes Willard."

Nanna shook Agnes's beefy hand. "It's nice to meet you, Agnes."

"It's my pleasure," Agnes murmured.

"Agnes and I are here because Beatrice Barker told us your husband wanted to hire us."

Nanna's slender brows lowered over pale, hazel eyes. "Really? Whatever for? I don't think the boys need a tutor." She laughed uneasily.

Flo smiled. "Actually, I'm not teaching anymore. I—that is—Agnes and I have an investigation business."

"Investigations?" Nanna's frown deepened. "I can't imagine what Dave was thinking."

"Has he been threatened? Or maybe someone is extorting money from him?"

The other woman shook her head. "Not that I know of. He's been a little—I don't know, jittery might be the right word. But I just put it down to what was going on at work." She shook her head. "I can't believe he didn't say something to me. This is terrible." Then her expression cleared. "Ah, I'll bet I know what he wanted to talk to you about. Those horrible activists."

"Activists?" Flo asked.

Nanna nodded. "Animal activists. They don't like the idea of raising chickens for food. They've been a constant presence here and at the plant. You probably passed them on the way in. We got a restraining order, so they mostly don't come onto the property anymore, but they never leave the front of the property these days." She sighed.

That probably explained the flyers on the road. "No activists. Maybe they went to pester Chisholm's for a while," Flo said, smiling.

Chisholm's Chickens was Potts Farms' rival in the area.

"Maybe." Nanna didn't return the smile. It was clear the activists had rattled her.

Flo reached out and clasped Nanna's hand. "It might be nothing. Maybe he just didn't want to worry you." Or maybe Bea was completely off her rocker. Flo certainly hoped her friend hadn't sent them on a wild goose chase. But if she had, it wouldn't hurt to give Dave Potts one of her cards while she was there.

"Is he home?"

"Dave? Yes. Or, at least he's around. I think he went out to the chicken coop a while ago." The frown returned to mar her attractive face. "My goodness, I think it's actually been a couple of hours now. I lose track of time when I'm in my gardens."

"Can we go speak to him?"

"Of course. Do you want me to show you the way?"

"That won't be necessary. You go on with your gardening. If you'll just point us in the right direction...?"

Nanna pointed past the big house. "There's a path through that small copse of evergreens there at the side of the house. It leads to the coop. It's a small, red building with white trim. You can't miss it."

Flo thanked the other woman. She and Agnes headed along the stone path leading from the paved driveway into the clump of old growth evergreens. They stepped into the grove and the scent of pine needles sweetened the stench permeating the air. Still, as they got closer, the smell only got worse.

Flo threw Agnes worried looks. "Something's not right. Do you smell that?"

Agnes gave Flo a blank look. "Smell what?"

"Seriously?"

That was when Flo noticed the slightly greasy aspect of Agnes's upper lip. "What's that on your face?"

Agnes's eyes went wide before she schooled her expression and turned away. "I don't know what you're talking about."

Flo reached up and ran her finger through the glob on Agnes's lip, holding it under her own nose. The purifying stench of mentholated ointment cooled her sinuses. "You're masking the smell with Dick's Vaporub!"

Agnes shoved her hands into her pockets. "I think I'm coming down with congestion. I'm just being careful."

"Careful my wrinkly patooty, you got an inside tip that it was going to be stinky here and didn't tell me."

Agnes's lips quivered. "I might have forgotten to tell you. That's not the same thing as deliberately not telling you."

"Isn't it?" Flo lifted an eyebrow at her friend. "What is it, some kind of bet? Who'd you bet that I'd wimp out and go running back to the car?"

Agnes barked out a laugh. "*If* there was a bet, and I'm not saying there was, who do you think it was?"

Flo stopped, her hands finding her hips as she glared at Agnes. "It had better not be Vlad or Morty." Morticia Newsome was the second half of the night manager duo and Vlad's coffin buddy. While Flo and Agnes had once helped Morty with a cult problem, the vampire queen still hated them and looked for every opportunity to cause them grief.

"Flo, do you really think I'd side with the enemy against you?"

Flo really didn't. But she never really knew with Agnes. All bets were off when Agnes was presented with a moral dilemma where pie or really any other food was involved. That thought sparked a revelation in Flo's brain. "It was Cook, wasn't it?"

Agnes barked out a laugh. "If it makes you feel better, I had to talk her into it. She took your side."

Flo shook her head. "You think you know people."

"Ah, don't be mad at Cook. She grew up around chicken farms. She hates them. Calls them 'those fowl things'. She didn't believe you'd scream like a girl and run away though." Agnes beamed. "That was me."

"What do you win if I run?"

"Two pies," Agnes responded happily.

"Good. I'm happy to deprive you of those pies," Flo said as they stepped out of the trees.

A beat later, she was really struggling to keep from letting Agnes win her bet.

CHAPTER THREE

HE WAS DRAPED OVER a bloody tree stump, or at least most of him was draped, the rest of him was lying on the ground next to the stump, eyes wide with surprise and mouth slack. The ax which had done the dirty deed was lying on the ground next to him, the blade still glossy with blood.

Agnes jerked to a stop beside Flo and made a small sound. One beefy hand flew to her mouth and she sucked air, then seemed to regret it and turned away, running screaming back down the path.

Flo dug her heels into the trampled grass and closed her eyes, breathing shallowly through her mouth and fighting to keep from being reintroduced to her lunch. Her mind swam to Cook's and Agnes's bet and her stomach rolled as she thought of pie.

She jerked her thoughts away and reached into her pocket, her eyes still closed. She clutched the phone in her hand, uncertain what to do next.

She should call 9-1-1.

She was obligated to report the murder.

But she'd have to open her eyes to punch in the numbers, and she was pretty sure she'd run screaming down the path if she did.

Flies buzzed busily around her and she retched, knowing why there were so many of them.

Poor Dave Potts. Poor Nanna. Poor David Junior and Pet. Flo knew the moment she made that call their worlds would change, exploding into horror.

Her hand tightened on the phone. She just needed a minute. Just one more minute to pull herself together.

Heavy footsteps sounded behind her and Flo's eyes jerked open before she could stop them. The world rolled with her stomach. Flo barely turned away in time to keep from hurling all over the crime scene.

She fell to her knees and retched into the greenery at the edge of the tree line. The footsteps stopped and waited, Flo pulled a tissue from her pocket and wiped her mouth. "I didn't run," she told Agnes in a rusty voice. "Or scream."

From somewhere down the path, Agnes called her name.

From. A. Distance.

Flo saw stars. Her head jerked around and she surged to her feet, stumbling a bit with dizziness. The path was empty. The gaze she'd felt watching her wasn't there.

More heavy footsteps approached and Agnes appeared through the trees. "Are you coming?"

Flo looked at her friend and then slid her gaze into the trees. "Were you just here a minute ago?"

Agnes frowned. "Um, yeah. Are you okay, Flo? You and I just walked out here together."

"No, I mean..." Flo approached her friend and grabbed her arm, looking back down the path and into the woods again. The wide, soft branches of the enormous pines danced on a soft breeze. Flo thought she saw a flash of white through the trees, but it was gone so fast she realized she must have imagined it. "Did you just walk up behind me a few seconds ago and then leave?"

"Why would I do that?"

Flo tightened her grip on Agnes's arm. "Did you see anybody else on the path?"

Agnes tugged her arm gently from Flo's grip, rubbing it as she frowned. "Of course not."

"You're sure?"

"Flo, this is hardly Grand Central Station. I think I'd have noticed one other person on the path." She cocked her head, dropping a heavy arm around Flo's shoulders. "You don't look so good. Let's go back to the house. We need to tell Mrs. Potts."

Flo shrugged Agnes off and shook her head. "I just want to look around first. Then we'll call Detective Peters and go talk to Nanna."

"I don't think..."

Flo didn't wait for her friend to finish that statement. She turned on her heel, very determinedly avoiding looking at what was left of Dave Potts on the stump. She circled around the stump, looking at the ground, one hand covering her nose.

A beat later, Agnes's big hand shot out in front of her. It was holding a small jar of ointment. Flo gratefully took the jar of Dick's Vapor Rub and slathered it under her nose. "Thanks."

"What are we looking for?" Agnes asked.

"I don't know." Flo pointed to some torn grass. "Those look like drag marks."

Agnes crouched down and ran her fingers along two wobbly tracks in the grass, six to eight inches apart. Her gaze slid toward the chicken coop. "They came from there."

Flo and Agnes followed the tracks to the small, red building, stopping in front of a door that stood slightly ajar. Flo used her arm to shove the door open, so as not to leave any prints and disrupt Detective Peters's crime scene. On that thought, she looked up at Agnes. "Don't touch anything."

Agnes gave a long-suffering sigh and shoved her hands into the pockets of her cotton shorts. She lifted a bushy brown eyebrow at Flo. "Happy?"

"I'll be happy if we come out of this building without you obliterating any evidence."

Shaking her head, Agnes stepped through the door and stopped, peering down at a large pile of chicken feed and bales of straw. "Nothing in here but supplies."

Flo squeezed in beside her friend and glanced around. The room was stifling hot, but there was a soft breeze coming from somewhere. She eyed the high, long windows just under the eaves and realized they were open a crack, allowing much-needed air into the small room.

She skimmed her gaze over the piles of supplies, stopping when she spotted a shovel leaning against the wall just behind the door. She walked over and looked at the garden tool, finding clay caked on its tip. Crouching down, Flo touched the mud and realized it was still moist. "This was used recently to dig." While she was down there, she saw something shiny behind the shovel, half buried in the dirt. She reached in and pulled out a necklace, the clasp missing.

She crouched there a moment, examining the plain gold chain. It was heavy and wide enough that it could have belonged to a man or a woman. Flo stood up and showed the jewelry to Agnes. "Look what I found."

"Maybe it belonged to the killer," Agnes speculated. "Potts might have pulled it off during a struggle."

Flo glanced around. "The drag marks do lead to this shed. Maybe he was killed here and then dragged out to the stump."

Agnes shrugged.

"Okay, I'm bringing this with me to show to Nanna. Let's go." Flo slipped the chain into the pocket of her slacks and motioned toward the door.

Agnes nodded. "With pleasure. I'm cooking in here."

Flo and Agnes started toward the door. Agnes was just about to step through into the hot sun beyond, when a large, threatening form suddenly filled the doorway, throwing a shadow into the small room and making Agnes jump and squeal in alarm.

What happened next was probably preordained by the gods of crime scene debauchery. Flo was starting to think Agnes was a supernatural being sent to earth to single-handedly destroy as many scenes as possible. No matter what anybody tried, nothing seemed to keep her from completing her appointed rounds.

Agnes came down hard on one foot and her ankle twisted, plunging her sideways with a grunt. Since she'd shoved her hands into her pockets to keep from touching anything, she had no way to catch herself when her shoulder hit the shovel leaning against the wall.

The shovel bounced off the wall and followed Agnes as she pinged back, clocking her hard between the eyes and sending her stumbling backward on a scream. She plodded heavily rearward, struggling to yank her hands out of her pockets as she fell over a bag of feed which had fallen partially into the aisle and, with a comical two-step that did nothing to slow the inevitable landing, slammed into the back wall with the force of a charging bull.

But the fun wasn't over.

Agnes crashed right through the wall, which admittedly had been made to contain creatures that weighed probably no more than a couple of pounds and was therefore not up to the task of withstanding a two-hundred-pound woman under momentum.

A chorus of alarmed squawks sounded as Agnes went through the wall and chicken feathers flew all around her as she crashed. Dust, feathers, and splintered lumber flew everywhere as Agnes landed with a wet splat that shot egg yolk in an arc around her.

She lay in the roost for a moment, blinking wildly as feathers filtered down and stuck to the gooey egg debris on her face.

Flo hurried over. "Are you okay?"

Agnes just kept blinking, her hands still struggling to extricate themselves from her shorts.

Flo's gaze swept the roost with alarm. "There are no chickens underneath you, are there, Agnes?"

Her friend shook her head and then sneezed several times, finally managing to yank one hand free to cover her face.

"Come on, hun. Let's get you out of there..."

A horrendous squawking noise interrupted Flo. She turned just in time to see an enormous bundle of beak, talons, and feathers bounding toward Agnes, rage writ large in every flapping inch.

Flo gave an alarmed squeal and covered her face with her arm just as the thing flew off the ground, beady eyes filled with hostile intent, and landed right on top of Agnes.

Her friend's shrieks brought Flo out of terrified inaction and she jumped into movement, grabbing the shovel Agnes had knocked into the aisle and swinging it at the attacking monster.

The enormous fowl took one last angry peck at Agnes and then squawked loudly before lifting its wings and fluttering away through the coop, into a grassy area filled with alarmed chickens.

Flo ducked her head through the broken wall and saw that the yard the chicken had escaped into was fenced and covered with chicken wire and a tarp for shade. Several other chickens ran squawking around the yard, no doubt discombobulated by having Agnes descend, literally, upon them while they were minding their own business.

She frowned. "How did that chicken get out of the yard?"

Agnes groaned, drawing Flo's gaze downward. Her friend was covered in blood from being scratched and pecked by the oversized bird. "Are you okay?"

Agnes's response was to try to struggle up off her back.

"Here," Flo said, grabbing her friend's arms. "Let me help."

With much grunting, sweating and a couple of near heart attacks, they finally managed to wrestle Agnes from the nest of her wreckage.

Red-faced and sweating, Agnes tugged her remaining hand from her pocket to the sound of ripping cotton. She grimaced, scrubbing her palms over the too-tight shorts. "My hands are sweaty. They got stuck."

"Mm-hm." Flo didn't want to point out that a bigger pair of shorts was probably in order. No sense hurting Agnes's feelings. Though Flo and their friends worried about Agnes's health. She'd already been diagnosed with high blood pressure.

"Let's get out of here," Flo said. "I want to check on Nanna and call Detective Peters." Then she grimaced, realizing they were going to have to admit that Agnes had debauched another crime scene. "I wonder if he'll believe the killer broke the wall?"

Agnes headed back out into the sunshine, her expression grave. "It was an accident. He'll just have to deal with it."

Flo sighed. "Yeah, I'm sure he'll deal with it just fine."

CHAPTER FOUR

"THAT WAS THE BIGGEST chicken I've ever seen," Agnes groused as she mopped at the scratches and peck marks on her fleshy arms with a clean tissue.

"That was no chicken," Flo clarified. "I think it might have been a rooster. Or a science experiment gone terribly wrong."

"Roosters are jerks," Agnes mumbled.

"Well, in his defense, you did crash into the roost and smash all those eggs." Flo watched Nanna Potts across the room. She was sitting on the couch in the living room of the big house, a soggy, well-used tissue in her hand as she nodded at something Detective Brent Peters asked her.

The aforementioned detective turned a murderous scowl her way and Flo gave him a smile, thinking it couldn't hurt. Though she had no doubt they were going to bear the brunt of his obvious unhappiness later, when there were no grieving widows around to witness it.

"I'm afraid there's no way Detective Peters is going to let us accompany him to the crime scene now that you've told him what happened," Flo said.

Agnes shrugged. "It was best he knew now. When he couldn't yell at us."

Flo's lips twitched upward. "Devious. But pure genius. I like it."

"If worse comes to worst, I'll take all the blame so he'll let you go with him."

Flo started to thank her friend, and then realized the implication behind her words. "But it *was* all your fault. What would I have to take the blame about?"

Agnes cocked a brow at her. "Whose idea was it to go into the shed?"

"Well, mine, but..."

"There ya go."

Flo didn't even know where to start with that. Using Agnes's reasoning, Flo was responsible for every crime scene debauching Agnes had been involved in. She narrowed her gaze at Agnes, noting the smug set to her jaw. "You're an evil genius, Agnes Willard."

Agnes snorted.

"Emphasis on evil."

The smirk fell away.

"Ladies. Can I speak with you both outside, please?"

Flo spun around and looked up at the detective's angry face. His expression was tight, but at least he was no longer frothing at the mouth, and his face had lost its eggplant-ish color.

Things were looking up.

They preceded him out the door and Peters closed it behind them, motioning toward the yard.

Flo noticed the three squad cars parked in the Potts's driveway and heard voices through the copse of evergreens. It seemed the detective had already dispatched uniforms to secure the crime scene.

She grimaced at the thought. What would they think when they saw the devastation in the chicken coop?

Flo stepped off the porch and headed toward the evergreens, thinking she might lure him there before he realized what she was doing.

"That's far enough, Mrs. Bee."

Oh, but it wasn't, Flo thought drearily. She gave him a forced smile. "I just wanted to get out of the sun."

He cocked a golden eyebrow at her. "Right. Okay, tell me everything that happened." He frowned in Agnes's direction. "Don't leave anything out."

"Well, Dave Potts was trying to get in touch with me about something," Flo began.

He held up a hand. "Wait. He was trying? You didn't actually speak to him?"

"I wish I had. He didn't know my number, so he was attempting to reach me through Silver Hills. But Vlad wouldn't put him through."

Peters' nodded, clearly understanding the dynamics there. He'd spent enough time at Silver Hills—and with Flo and Co.—to know all about Vlad. Even if he bypassed a lot of the urban legend they'd created around the Newsomes, Peters understood that Vlad was focused solely on self-aggrandizement, and that he was selfish and mean-spirited to the extreme. The last thing Vladwicke Newsome would ever want to do was help a man whom he considered a rival.

"You don't know what he was trying to contact you about?"

"Only that it was about an investigation."

Interest lit the young cop's gaze. "Given what's happened, that puts a new emphasis on this case."

Flo nodded. "Somebody might have been threatening him. Nanna said he'd been a bit jittery lately."

The detective's eyes narrowed. "You interviewed the witness before calling me?"

"Of course not," Flo said, losing patience with his territorial demeanor. "Agnes and I came to the house looking for Potts. Nanna was gardening. She sent us to the coop to find him."

Peters nodded, looking thoughtful for a moment. Then he drew himself up, pulling air into his lungs as if trying to prepare for something.

He swung his gaze to Agnes, rather reluctantly Flo thought.

"Okay, Ms. Willard. Tell me what you saw when you went back there."

Agnes skimmed Flo a surprised look. Clearly, she hadn't been expecting to be grilled directly about the debauchery inside the coop. If Flo knew her friend, Agnes had been carefully building her story, thick with excuses for why everything had happened the way it had. She didn't usually give him the details of a scene.

Finally, she shrugged as if accepting the challenge and pointed down the path. "We walked through there. I was telling Flo about the bet Cook and I had that she'd scream like a girl and run away..."

Peters held up a hand. "You already knew about the murder and you discussed it with Cook?"

"No. Try to stay with me, Detective."

When he bristled, Flo hurried to explain. "They thought the smell of chicken poop would be too much for me."

His brows peaked in surprise. "They don't know you very well, do they, Mrs. Bee?"

Flo chuckled. "Cook does. She was having none of it. But Agnes was hoping for a pie, so she was willing to give it a try." Which reminded Flo, she'd have to ask her friend later what she had to do for Cook for losing.

"Anyway," Agnes interrupted, giving Flo a long-suffering look. "We came out of the woods and saw..." She swallowed hard. "Um—Mr. Potts." Agnes swallowed again. "Um, he was..." She covered her mouth as her throat worked.

"He was draped over a tree stump and his head was cut off," Flo said, grimacing. "Like a chicken."

Even Peters grimaced at that. "Brutal. That kind of killing screams rage."

"Yes," Flo agreed. "And I don't think you can ignore the significance of the chickens either."

"I agree. Mrs. Potts said he'd gone back to slaughter one of them for dinner."

"Then he was probably in the process of killing one when he was attacked?" Flo asked, frowning. "That might rule out premeditation."

"Agreed. And if it's a crime of passion," he began.

"Then we need to look at Nanna too." Flo's stomach twisted at the idea. But the statistics on spouses murdering each other were well documented.

They stood in silence for a long moment and then Peters looked at Agnes. "What happened after you saw the body?"

"She ran screaming down the path like a girly-girl," Flo said happily.

Agnes crossed beefy arms over her chest and scowled down at Flo.

The young detective struggled not to grin. "You didn't touch the body or the weapon, did you?"

"No," Flo assured him. "We gave it a wide berth. It was too disturbing to even look at."

"Good. At least I can preserve the evidence *there*." He put his hands on his hips. "Now tell me about the chicken coop."

Agnes opened her mouth but was interrupted before she could begin with her concocted story.

Heavy footsteps plodded down the path toward them, and a rotund, hairy bear of a sweat-glazed man trudged out of the trees. Officer Jason a.k.a. Meanie Meldick's gaze swung right to Agnes and his fleshy lips curved upward. He swiped a thick arm, covered in a dense pelt of dark hair, over his greasy face and tugged on his overstretched blue uniform shirt as if trying to make himself presentable.

Flo grabbed her friend's wrist to hold her there as she dug her size eleven sneakers into the turf and prepared to make a run for it. "Stay strong," she whispered. "I'll protect you."

Agnes moved slightly sideways, putting Flo's five feet two inch, one hundred and fifteen-pound form between her and the massive uniformed officer.

Flo gulped loudly. She was in grave danger of becoming the thoroughly inadequate filling in a Meldick-Willard sandwich.

An extremely unappetizing thought.

"Detective," Meldick announced in his booming voice. "I think you need to come see this." Though he clearly spoke to

Detective Peters, his bulging brown gaze never left Agnes. He gave her a disturbing leer that was probably meant to be a smile.

Peters started off down the path and Meldick lumbered along beside him, his fleshy hands waving around him as he presumably explained what they'd discovered. He spoke in an uncharacteristically quiet tone that was hard for Flo to hear as they hurried toward the scene.

Flo didn't dare get close enough to listen since she was hoping the detective wouldn't notice them following along. She needed to find out what Meldick was so excited about before Peters noticed her and sent them packing.

The two men emerged from the tree line, and Agnes started to step out after them. Flo grabbed her arm. "Hang back. Maybe he won't notice we're here," she said in an urgent whisper.

Agnes nodded and the two of them stepped sideways by unspoken agreement, letting the draping limbs of the trees provide a little cover.

Flo was happy to see that the body was gone. Or, she realized, not gone but at least no longer draped over the stump. There was a gurney off to the side that held a heavy black bag which Flo assumed contained Dave Potts' remains.

Meldick pointed to something on the ground on the other side of the stump. Peters picked his way along the ground, taking care not to step into the torn grass surrounding the scene. Bright yellow evidence markers marked the spot where Potts's feet had dug into the earth.

Flo grimaced, hoping he hadn't suffered overly before he died. She wouldn't wish his kind of death on anyone.

The detective crouched down and studied the ground behind the stump. Flo found herself stepping forward, trying to see what he was looking at.

But she was too short, the stump was too high, and it was too far away. Flo frowned in frustration.

A tree limb across the path snapped back with a whoosh and Flo jumped, pressing a hand against her chest as a uniformed cop walked out of the woods. The young, dark-haired cop saw them and waved, smiling.

Flo recognized Officer Nicholas Bachus. The twenty-something cop had probably been smoking in the woods. Nasty habit.

But Flo's thoughts quickly slid away from the uniformed officer. She was remembering something she needed to tell Detective Peters.

"Stay here," she told Agnes in a stern tone. Flo stepped out of the trees. "Detective Peters," she called out, stepping well around the scene like he had. "I remembered something you need to know." She moved quickly, hoping to catch a glimpse of whatever was on the ground before he slipped it into the evidence bag he held in his hand.

Peters straightened and threw up a hand. "Stop right there, Mrs. Bee! You're going to defile my crime scene again."

She stepped sideways, throwing up her hands as if to indicate that she had no intention of doing any such thing. "I'm staying well out of the area," she told him.

Peters motioned to someone behind Flo. She turned to see another detective strolling toward them, a big roll of crime scene tape in his hand.

Detective Thomas Nightshade grimaced when he saw her. "Mrs. Bee, I should have known you and your sidekick would be here. You just can't resist a chance to snoop around a murder, can you?"

Agnes frowned. "Hey! How come I have to be the sidekick?"

Flo cast a wary gaze over the movie-star handsome detective. As usual, his white-blond hair was combed straight back from an unlined forehead, perfectly coiffed above pretty blue eyes. "Detective. I'm afraid you've got it backward. Agnes and I found Mr. Potts. I called it in."

Nightshade slid a surprised look to Peters. The young detective nodded. "It's true. They did find him first. And you'll see proof of that when you go into the chicken coop there and see the results of their, 'investigating.'"

Flo pinched her lips with irritation. "Anyway—I needed to tell you something I'd forgotten. I believe that when Agnes and I first arrived the murderer was still here."

"Why do you think that?" Peters asked.

"Because there was someone in the woods with us. I heard whoever it was come up behind me, but when I turned around he was gone. I just caught a flash of something white disappearing through the woods."

Peters and Nightshade shared a look. Then Nightshade offered her a condescending glance. "You were probably just upset and imagined it."

"No, she didn't," Agnes said from behind me. "I think I heard somebody too."

Both detectives and Flo swung around at the same time, all three throwing up their hands as Agnes lumbered right for the stump.

"No!" they yelled in unison.

But it was too late, Agnes cocked her head in question, as her leg stretched out and her foot smacked down into soggy dirt. Her sneaker hit a blood-saturated patch of mud and started to slide.

There was a beat of suspended motion, where Agnes's eyes went round and her mouth opened in dismay. Then the suspension folded in and action resumed, propelling Agnes forward into everybody's worst nightmare.

The two cops started forward but it was too late. All anybody could do was watch in horror as Agnes's foot slid out from under her and she stumbled forward, arms wind-milling wildly as she tried to regain her balance.

But balance was not restored.

Agnes did two final, mincing steps and then spun a complete circle, arms akimbo, before tripping over the outside edge of the sawed-off tree and landing hard across the stump with a resounding "umph" sound.

That was the point that gravity and momentum took up the baton.

Agnes's arms swung downward, belatedly, in an attempt to protect her from the fall. Her hand smacked down hard, hitting the handle of the ax lying next to the sawed-off base of the tree and sending it into air. The ax spun wildly for a second and then, its upward mobility finally spent, the murder weapon began a downward trajectory, finally embedding itself into the side of the stump. It vibrated there for a beat and then the handle slowly descended downward, softly thwacking into the saturated mud alongside the tree, a yellow evidence marker perched jauntily atop its handle like an unfortunate party hat.

Everything went still and silent. Disbelieving gazes bulged in witness of the disaster. All voices were locked into silence. And somewhere, buried deep beneath Flo's best intentions, a tiny speck of glee reared its ugly head.

She was pretty sure Peters might finally understand the unstoppable force that was Agnes Willard.

CHAPTER FIVE

"I DON'T THINK I'VE ever seen him that mad before," Agnes told Flo as she limped into Silver Hills.

Flo shuddered. "For a minute there, I thought he was going to shoot you."

"I know, right?" Agnes said, appalled. "I couldn't believe he pulled his gun like that."

"Thank goodness Detective Nightshade was there to stop him," Flo agreed. "And believe me, I never thought I'd be happy that Nightshade was there."

But despite their nearly sending poor Detective Peters into a straitjacket in a padded room, Flo was happy. Because in all the commotion, she'd gotten a look at the evidence Meanie and Peters had been perusing and had taken a quick picture of it with her phone. She couldn't wait to enlarge the picture and figure out what she had.

TC hurried up to them as they entered the lobby. Her tall, slender frame was covered in the usual light-weight tee shirt and yoga pants, and she had her long, dark locks pulled back into a perky ponytail. "Hey, ladies."

"Hi, TC," Flo said, giving her friend a smile and an impulsive hug. "How are you?"

TC's answering smile was filled with real pleasure. "I'm good. Busy as always. Are you two coming to swim aerobics later?"

Flo grimaced. The water classes weren't her favorite. She'd never really enjoyed swimming. Though she supposed kicking her legs and swinging her arms while standing in water up to her armpits didn't really count as swimming. "If there's no way to get out of it."

TC laughed. "I'm counting on you to round out the class. Besides, Roger's going to be there, and he'll be very disappointed if you don't show up."

Roger Attles was Flo's heartthrob and one of the kindest, most handsome men she knew. She surely didn't want to disappoint Roger. "You drive a hard bargain but, I'll be there."

TC nodded. "Good." She glanced at Agnes for verification and then flinched. "Oh my gosh! What happened to you, Agnes? You look like you've been run over by a tiller."

Agnes nodded enthusiastically. "I might as well have been. I was attacked by a freakishly big chicken."

TC's mouth came open as she prepared to respond, then it slammed shut again when she realized she had no response. She turned a questioning glance to Flo.

"It's true," Flo verified. "We went to see Dave Potts."

"What? Why?" TC asked. Then she held up a hand. "Never mind. I don't need to know." She gave them a sad smile and wiggled her fingers in a wave. "I'll see you both in an hour?"

"I'm not sure chlorine would be good for my cuts," Agnes said.

"Oh, okay," TC said agreeably. "You're probably right. I hope you feel better soon." Their friend gave Flo a sad look and then turned away, heading toward her office.

Flo sighed. "I hate this."

Agnes rubbed her scratched up arms. "Why don't you just tell her you don't want to go swimming."

Shaking her head, Flo started toward the elevator. She'd run up and take her dog, Rodney out for a pee then get ready for aerobics. "Not that. She's right. If I don't go Roger will be unhappy."

"Heaven knows we can't let Roger be unhappy," Agnes mumbled as she stabbed a heavy finger onto the *Up* button.

Flo eyed her for a moment and then decided to let it go. Her friend was cranky and she didn't blame her. She'd had quite a day.

They stepped into the elevator and Flo waited for the doors to close. "I just hate seeing Tricia so unhappy."

"She could stop being unhappy if she'd just join the fun again."

Flo shrugged.

"Honestly, I don't see what the problem is. She's not even dating Detective Killjoy anymore. She might as well help us figure out who killed Potts."

The door opened on Flo's floor. She started out of the elevator and then realized Agnes wasn't following. She turned back. "Coming?"

"No. I'm going to go home. I need to feed Tolstoy." Tolstoy, a.k.a. the grim reaper, was Agnes's giant orange striped cat. He'd gotten a reputation as the reaper because he seemed drawn to people who were dying. He liked to sit on them and bathe his paws as if he were doing them a favor by ushering them into the next life.

Sadness swept through Flo. Was she losing Agnes too? "But I have a picture of the evidence. Don't you want to see what it is?"

Agnes stabbed the button for the third floor, where she lived. "You can show it to me in the morning. Night, Flo."

The door slid closed.

"Night," Flo whispered to the closed door. Rodney was waiting for her at the door, his long dachshund form wagging with his skinny tail.

Flo smiled. "Hello, handsome. At least you still love me, don't you?"

The elderly doxie licked her hand and tried to shove past her into the hallway. Flo laughed. "Or you need to potty and I'm just a convenient way to make that happen." She sighed. Grabbing Rodney's leash off the hook near the door, Flo clipped it on and they headed for the stairwell. She had to nearly run down the flight of stairs trying to keep up with her short-legged dog. She pushed the door open on level one and exited into the sweet-smelling night.

The side of the building where Flo took her dog for his potty visits was covered in beautiful, vining red roses. The wonderful scent of the flowers permeated the area as Flo and Rodney struck out for the grassy area that bordered the parking lot. Flo liked that particular spot because of the roses, but also because the parking lot back there was fairly quiet and she felt safe letting Rodney off leash to wander around.

And since the short-haired, red doxie was almost fifteen years old, she was pretty sure she could catch him if he took off running. Though, she was probably kidding herself. He might be fifteen in dog years, but he was still a spunky toddler in attitude years.

"I thought I'd find you out here, doll."

Flo looked up with a smile. "Hello, Roger." She accepted a gentle peck on the cheek, squeezing his arm with affection. "What are you up to this beautiful evening?"

Roger was tall and slender, almost gangly. He had intelligent blue eyes that sparkled with humor more often than they filled with worry or anger. He shoved his long fingers through a thick mop of silver hair and shook his head. "I missed you at dinner." Roger reached into the pocket of his light gray tracksuit and pulled something out that was wrapped in a napkin. "I figured you must be embroiled in some new intrigue, so I brought you a cookie."

Tears burned Flo's eyes. She looked away so he wouldn't see them. "You are such a wonderful man," she said, her voice thick with the unshed tears.

"Hey, doll." He sat down on the bench next to her and dropped an arm around her shoulders, pulling her close. "What's wrong?"

Flo let her head rest on his shoulder. "I found a body today."

"Oh no." He kissed her on the temple. "I'm sorry. I'm sure that was very disturbing. Who was it?"

She sniffled. "Dave Potts."

She felt his confusion in his silence. Glancing up, she clarified. "It was pretty gruesome. And, of course, Agnes debauched the scene. Twice."

Roger whistled softly. "That's an overachievement even for her."

Flo found herself chuckling. "You couldn't be more right. And the second time she did it right in front of Detective Peters."

Roger's blue eyes went wide. "Oh my."

"Yes." Flo shook her head. "I thought he might do violence to her."

Roger rubbed her arm and they sat in silence for a moment, watching Rodney sniff his way around a small bush, tail whipping the air happily behind him.

Finally, Roger reached for Flo's hand and lifted it to his lips, kissing the back of it before pressing it against his heart. "Now, how about you tell me what's really bothering you?"

Flo gave him an unsteady smile. "You know me too well."

"It's my life's goal."

She couldn't help laughing, feeling like a silly school girl. He had that effect on her. It was one of the things she loved most about him. "It's TC."

Roger nodded. He didn't look surprised. "She's still keeping her distance?"

"Yes. But I can tell she's miserable. And now Agnes seems to be pulling away too." Flo frowned. "She didn't even want to look at my new evidence."

"Well, to be fair, Agnes has had a really bad day."

"Yes, she certainly has. But she's usually not bothered by those things."

"Don't believe that for a minute," Roger told her. "Agnes is bothered by every single thing. She just puts on a strong front.

She pretends she's impermeable, thinking if she believes it, and she can make everyone else believe it, she can make it true."

"Do you really think so?"

"I know so, doll."

"Agnes has been my best friend for almost three years. How is it you understand her better than I do?"

He squeezed the hand he held against his chest. "Because I see her when she lets her guard down. She never lets it down when you're around, doll. She admires you too much. She wants to be like you. But everything she does is like Agnes and nothing like you."

"That's so sad."

"It can be. But I don't really believe that Agnes is sad. I think she takes each event she faces as a challenge which she intends to beat. She's a genuinely impressive human being, doll. And I'm not just blowing smoke. I truly believe that."

Flo rested her head on his shoulder and gave a sigh. "Okay, since you're so good at this, tell me what to do about TC."

He didn't respond for a moment and Flo thought he wasn't going to. She lifted her head and looked up at him. Roger was staring at Rodney, but he turned when he felt her gaze. "Can I tell you a little secret?"

"Please."

"I think TC's waiting for you to invite her back into the sewing circle."

Flo stared at him in shock. He couldn't possibly be right. Finally, she shook her head. "I disagree, Roger. She's made it clear that she wants nothing to do with my little intrigues. And, if her relationship with Detective Peters was the cause of her pulling away, she no longer has that excuse. They've broken up."

"They have. But I wouldn't count on that lasting. I've seen the way those two young people look at each other. They'll be back together soon."

Frustration made Flo bite back a sigh. "That's good for them, at least."

He looked down at her, his lips quivering. "But not for you?"

Shrugging, Flo gently tugged her hand free and unwrapped the gingerbread cookie he'd given her, breaking off a tender bite. "I want TC to be happy."

"But you wish she could be happy with the detective as well as with you."

"Yes." She looked up into his warm blue gaze. "Is that wrong?"

"Not at all. And I believe TC can walk that line. But she can't seem to take the first step in that direction. She needs your help for that."

"You think I should confront her?" Flo grimaced at the thought.

"Confront is the wrong word. But if you went to her and told her you needed her help, you'd give her the excuse she needs to relent."

Flo chewed another bite, thinking. After a moment she realized he might be right. She nodded. "I'll talk to her tonight, after aerobics."

Roger patted her knee and stood up. "Good. And I want to hear all about Dave Potts. But right now, I have to go get ready for some water aerobics." He waggled dark silver eyebrows and Flo giggled like a school girl again. "I'll see you in a bit."

Rodney wandered up as Flo was popping the last bite of cookie into her mouth. "Are you ready to go have your dinner, little man?"

The chubby dachshund barked enthusiastically and bounced toward the building. She didn't bother trying to catch him as he made a run for the door. She'd clip the leash on him before they started up the steps. There was never anyone else in the stairwell at that time of night, so Flo didn't think she needed to worry about the opinionated doxie nibbling on anybody's calves before she could grab him.

She couldn't have been more wrong.

CHAPTER SIX

THE SIDE DOOR OPENED when Flo was still several feet away.

Rodney flew through the door on a growl and a shrill scream pierced the otherwise calm night.

The door slammed shut again.

"Oh no!" Flo took off running. As she reached for the handle, she grimaced at the sounds of growling and scuffling, peppered by the occasional shrill yelp of alarm.

She jerked the door open and saw a dark-haired woman who was fending Flo's little dachshund off with her oversized purse. The woman's gaze shot to hers and a pleading light filled her green eyes.

Flo dove in. "Rodney, no!" She grabbed his collar and yanked him backward as TC retreated up a couple of steps with her fang-dented leather purse still held out like a shield. Flo clipped the leash onto her dog's collar. "Are you all right, hun?"

TC dropped down onto the step and shoved a dark ribbon of hair out of her eyes, laughing breathlessly. "I'm fine. The little stinker surprised me though."

Flo wagged her finger at Rodney, who wagged his tail back in response, perfectly happy with his adventure. "I swear, I don't know what gets into him sometimes."

TC reached into her purse and pulled out something wrapped in a napkin. "I didn't see you at dinner so I thought I'd bring you a cookie."

Flo stared at the cookie for a long moment and then burst into laughter. She leaned against the door, holding her stomach as hilarity overcame her. She didn't know why she found it so funny. Judging by the confused look on TC's face, her friend didn't understand it either. She made a concerted effort to get control of herself and took a deep breath. "I'm sorry, hun. I just think that's the sweetest thing."

TC's frown deepened.

"Roger just did exactly the same thing. I have the best friends in the world."

TC's frown finally cleared, and she gave Flo an embarrassed smile. "Oh. Well." She shoved the cookie back into her big purse.

"But I'm still a bit hungry. Would you like to share the cookie? I could make us some tea?"

"I'd really like that," TC said.

Flo nodded, beaming at her friend. "I'm glad." Then she blinked. "Oh, water aerobics."

TC shook her head. "Cancelled. That's one of the reasons I came looking for you. I made an announcement on the intercom, but Roger told me you were outside and probably hadn't heard it."

Flo's brows lifted. *Roger*! That devil. He'd sent TC out with an ulterior motive. "What happened?"

TC shrugged, a grin playing on her face. "The YMCA won't let us come back because the last time we were there Old Mrs. Peoples peed in the pool and then bragged about it to the towel girl."

Alarm brought Flo's eyes wide. "She did what, now? I was standing right next to her." Flo cast her mind back to the week before, trying to remember if she'd experienced any warm spots. She might not have noticed at the time. With Old Mrs. Peoples only a couple of feet away, she'd been more concerned about floating objects of the more solid variety happening.

TC winced. "Yup. Sorry." She stood up and turned, starting up the stairs.

Flo followed, keeping Rodney on a short lead. She needn't have bothered. He was too busy chasing bits of leaf and other debris out of the corners of the steps to care about TC. In his Napoleon-like mind, she'd already been conquered. There were gum wrappers and dead bugs that still needed subduing.

"COOK MAKES THE BEST gingerbread," Flo said as she settled her half of the oversized cookie back onto a napkin.

TC sipped her tea, nodding. "Don't tell anybody but this is my second one." She gave Flo a guilty smile. "And I'm not working out either. I'm totally letting myself go."

There was something sad in the way her friend said it that made Flo reach across the table and briefly clasp her hand. "How have you been, Tricia? I haven't seen much of you lately."

TC pressed her finger into the crumbs on her napkin. She hesitated a long moment before responding to Flo's question. "I miss him."

That wasn't the response Flo had been expecting. She was at a loss for a beat, then she patted TC's hand. "Well, if that man doesn't recognize what a wonderful woman you are, he doesn't deserve you."

"I keep telling myself that."

"And does your self believe you?"

TC chuckled. "Almost."

"Well, it's absolutely true. Look what you were willing to do to make it work. You even stopped hanging with your friends because it annoyed him." Flo was appalled at the bitter tone in her words. She hadn't realized until that moment that she was a little bit peeved about TC's abandonment.

TC's gaze rose to hers. "I didn't do that for him."

Flo felt her face heat with hurt. She sipped her tea to cover it.

"I mean, I did, but not for the reasons you think. Helping you investigate, going behind his back, made me feel like I was betraying him. It felt wrong, Flo. I hope you can understand that?"

"I can. But we're your friends."

The hurt tone in Flo's words hung between them for a second, painful but necessary. If Roger was right and TC needed to hear Flo's feelings on the matter, she didn't know any other way to get that across to TC. She had to be brutally honest. "You did hurt my feelings, hun. I won't lie to you. But the thing that hurt the most was that you had to choose at all. He should never have asked you for that. And then in the end, you aren't together anyway."

TC ripped tiny pieces off her napkin, avoiding Flo's gaze. They sat with Flo's admission anchoring the silence until TC sighed. "I made a complete mess of it all, didn't I?"

"Not a complete mess," Flo said, smiling gently.

TC chuckled and some of the tension leached from the air. She reached across and squeezed Flo's hand. "I'm so sorry I hurt you."

Flo shook her head, dismissively. Then she had an idea. "Would you like to make it up to me?"

"What did you have in mind?"

"I could actually use your help on something."

TC frowned. "Dave Potts?"

"How'd you know?"

"I didn't really. But I saw that he was murdered and I saw Agnes's condition when you came back to the residence today."

They shared a grin.

"She debauched another crime scene, didn't she?" TC asked.

"Twice. You should have seen it, TC. It was epic."

They laughed companionably.

"I thought Detective Peters was going to shoot her."

TC's smile dimmed. Flo hurried ahead with her request before she lost TC to her emotions again. "I snapped a picture of some evidence and I could use your help identifying it."

"What is it?" TC leaned closer as Flo scrolled through her pictures and enlarged the ones she'd quickly snapped at the scene. The first one she found was a picture mostly of Officer Meldick's muddy boot.

Flo flushed with embarrassment. "I had to snap fast and I wasn't looking right at it because I didn't want Meanie Meldick to know what I was doing."

"Meanie was there?" TC asked, her eyes sparkling. "What did Agnes think about that?"

"She tried to make a run for it but I stopped her. I'm pretty sure he'll be over his crush though after seeing her obliterate their crime scene," Flo said, grimacing.

"I wouldn't count on it."

Flo found the picture she'd been looking for and enlarged it, shoving it toward TC. "It looks really familiar to me, but I can't quite place it. Can you?"

The picture was of a tiny piece of paper, triangular shaped with a ragged edge on one side. It looked like the corner of a flyer or something. The color of the scrap was mostly obscured by mud spatters, but Flo thought it could be dark red. There was a slash of white where the corner had been torn away, like the loop of a letter.

TC studied it for a long moment as Flo waited. Finally, she nodded. "I have seen this before." Her head shot up. "You know what this looks like?"

Flo shook her head.

"Vlad's new flyers. He hasn't spread them around yet, but I saw them yesterday on his desk."

"Oh no," Flo's stomach twisted. "That's not good, TC. He'll be blamed for Potts's murder. Everybody knows they hated each other. And with Potts out of the race, Vlad is running unopposed."

"I agree. It will be bad. If I'm right. But, I could be wrong. I only saw the flyers once and not for long. When he saw me looking, Vlad grabbed the stack and shoved them into the center drawer of his desk."

Flo glanced at the clock. "There's only one way to find out."

TC's eyes sparkled with excitement. "You mean...?"

"Yes. We need to search his office. Are you game?"

TC only hesitated for a beat. Then it was all Flo could do to keep up with her friend as she nearly ran toward the door.

They were going into the vampire's lair!

CHAPTER SEVEN

STANDING IN THE SHADOWS under the staircase lead-ing to the second level, Flo waved at the woman who cleaned her apartment. Maria waved back, pointing up the stairs and showing Flo the clean sheets she carried. Flo gave her the thumbs up.

"It must be nice having someone put clean sheets on your bed every week and clean your house for you," TC said.

"Perks of getting old, hun," Flo said, smiling. "I cleaned my own house for decades. When Richard offered the service for a few more dollars a month, I jumped at it."

"Hopefully the devil with short legs won't eat her."

Flo smacked TC lightly on the arm. "My darling little man adores Maria. It's just you he hates."

"And Agnes."

"And Agnes."

"And just about everybody else."

Flo narrowed her gaze on TC. "Okay, you might be right. But he *does* like Maria. I think it's the accent. He just sits there, cocking his head at her when she talks. It's cute."

TC chuckled, "Yeah, adorable." She moved out of the shadows a bit so she could see the vamps better. They were standing in the dining room, brow-beating poor Cook about something.

"They're probably mad she didn't serve blood pudding for dessert," TC muttered.

Flo chuckled.

After a moment, Flo stepped out of the shadows and waved to get Cook's attention. When the big woman's gaze snapped her way, Flo motioned toward the kitchen.

Flo prayed the other woman got her meaning or she'd have to send TC in to lure the Newsomes off.

Cook frowned mightily, but they watched her swing a meaty arm toward the kitchen and then stalk off in that direction.

Morty and Vlad shared a look and drifted into motion behind her. As they moved, the overhead lights flickered and the music playing softly through the overhead speakers stuttered.

As soon as they disappeared through the swinging kitchen door, Flo and TC hurried across the nearly empty lobby.

Flo's gaze swung around as she hurried after TC, whose long strides ate up the floor twice as fast as Flo's.

Thankfully, they were able to duck through the office door before anyone spotted them. Flo closed the door quietly behind them and locked it.

At TC's raised brow, she shrugged. "It'll buy us some time to grab pitchforks if the vamps attack."

TC grinned. "Come on."

They hurried past the messy desk where Morticia held court in the front office and entered the darkened Manager's office.

In contrast to his wife's desk, Vlad's was spotless, with nary a piece of paper or a speck of dust in sight when they flipped on the light.

"It's easy to see who does all the work in that duo," Flo mumbled.

Shaking her head, TC scanned a look back to Morty's desk. "You know, that's always bothered me. She doesn't strike me as the type to play the little woman. Why does he get the big office and she gets the old desk in the front office?"

"Whoever sits at that desk has to deal with people. She might be afraid he'd drain everyone dry who came through the door."

TC dragged her gaze away from Morty's desk, shrugging. "Who am I to second-guess vampire mating habits?"

"Ugh!" Flo said, shuddering. "Please, never use the word mating in a discussion about the vamps again."

Grinning unrepentantly, TC hurried across the office and circled around behind Vlad's desk. She tugged on the center drawer. It didn't move. "Locked. Dangit!"

"Can you unlock it?" Flo asked.

"I'm not sure. Give me a minute to think."

Flo nodded. "I'll see if there's a flyer on Morty's desk."

Flo was shuffling through the paper mountain in the center of Morty's desk when the knob to the exterior door started to turn.

She slammed the papers she'd been shuffling back down to the desk and hurried over to the interior door. "They're back!" she whispered harshly to TC.

TC hurried back around the desk and pulled the door closed behind her. "Let me take the lead on this."

Flo was happy to let TC take the lead since she had no idea how to explain their presence there.

A soft knock sounded on the door.

Flo and TC shared a look. If the vamps had returned, they'd be pounding angrily on the door.

"Doll, open the door."

Roger!

Flo turned the lock and opened the door just as Vlad arrived.

"There you are," Roger said loudly. "Did you get the application?"

"What's going on here?" Vlad boomed.

Behind him, lights flickered and faces turned to see which unsuspecting villager was about to be drained.

TC slipped past Flo at the door. She glared at Vlad. "No need to bellow, Vlad. I just came to tell you we need to find a new venue for the water aerobics. The YMCA has kicked us to the curb."

"It's all nonsense anyway," Vlad said in his oily voice. "Just pick some other equally pedestrian and low-class activity. The hoards don't care what they're doing. They're just looking for a moment's reprieve from their debilitatingly mundane lives."

"Why Vlad, that's almost poetic. It's nice to know you have such a high opinion of the residents," Flo said.

He lifted a too-slender black eyebrow, his eyes colder than the North Pole in December. "You weren't aware of my feelings? Perhaps I need to be more succinct. I believe you're all idiots."

Roger moved closer, his hands fisting at his sides. He towered over the diminutive Vlad, and the rage radiating off him made even the reprehensible manager take a step back. "Are you forgetting that all these wonderful people you call idiots will vote in the mayoral race, *Vladwicke*." He said the other man's name as if it were a chunk of dog doo on his tongue. "They have families who vote. Friends who vote. Acquaintances who vote. You might want to at least pretend you don't despise them."

Vlad shrugged. "I guess you haven't heard, Attles. Potts is dead. I have no competition."

"I had heard," said Roger. "In my days as a lawyer, that would be seen as motive. I surely hope you didn't have anything to do with Potts's death, Newsome. Because, if you did, I'm going to make darn sure the city has the best prosecutor money can buy to prove it."

He wrapped an arm around Flo's shoulders. "Come on, doll. I'll buy you an adult beverage. I need something to wash the stain of politician from my psyche."

"NOW, TELL ME ABOUT Potts," Roger requested as they sipped their red wine. They'd intended to go to the bar area at Silver Hills, which was adjacent to the dining room, but decided against it when they saw all the curious gazes pointed their way.

Roger had kindly invited TC to come along with them to *Gioppino's Italian Restaurant*. The cozy eatery had been a favorite place to eat even before they'd learned their friend Celia Angonetti and her husband Massimo owned it.

Flo sipped her wine and glanced toward TC, lifting her eyebrows in question.

TC sighed. "Go ahead. I have a feeling I'm going to get dragged into this. You might as well tell me all about it now."

TC's carefully crafted disgust was belied by the interest in her gaze. Flo skimmed Roger a look and he winked, smiling.

He'd been right. TC had been waiting for an invitation to join the fun. The man was just too smart for his own good.

"Well, it all started with Elisa Kemp," Flo began.

"Doesn't it always?" TC asked, spurring a chuckle from Roger.

"She came up to me this morning and told me Dave Potts had been trying to get hold of me about some business. I asked her how she knew and she said that Bea had..."

"Bea Barker?" Roger interrupted.

"Yes. Apparently, Bea overheard Vlad shutting Potts down on the phone. So I spoke to her, and she said my name was mentioned and that Vlad seemed to be trying to keep Potts away from me. Or at least was unwilling to help us connect. Well, you can imagine that got my interest..."

TC and Roger both made exaggerated exclamations of shock and Flo gave them her best substitute teacher glare. "Pipe down, you two." She shook her head. "Agnes and I drove out to Potts's house."

TC leaned forward excitedly. "What's it like? I've heard he has—had—more money than a Hollywood A-Lister."

"It was very nice," Flo agreed. "But very homey. I'm sure that's Nanna's influence. She's a very nice woman. I actually taught their two kids back in the day. I've kind of known the family for a while."

"What were the kids like?" Roger asked.

Flo didn't like the direction his agile mind was already going. "You mean, is it possible either of them killed their father? It's possible of course. But I'd say unlikely. They're both pursuing lucrative careers and live in other towns."

"You and Agnes went to the house..." TC spurred.

"Dave wasn't there, but we spoke to Nanna. She was working in her garden."

"Where was he?" Roger asked.

"In the chicken coop. It was through a small woods, maybe a city block's distance from the house."

Roger narrowed his gaze. "His wife was working in the garden a mere block away and didn't hear anything?"

Flo shrugged. She understood how Roger was seeing the whole thing. Everybody who knew anything at all about crime knew that victims were usually killed by an acquaintance. Often the spouse. "I know what you're thinking, Roger. But the woods would have dampened a lot of sound. And the way he was killed..." Flo just couldn't visualize Nanna hacking at her husband with an ax. "I can't see a woman doing that."

"Do I want to know?" TC asked, wincing.

"Probably not. But in for a penny..."

"In for a pound," TC sighed out. "Okay, let's hear the gory details."

"No gory details. The big picture is gory enough. He was draped over a tree stump which has probably been used in the past to slaughter chickens." She swallowed hard at the memory. "Let's just say that a very important part of him was lying on the ground next to an ax."

TC's eyes grew to the size of golf balls. "Oh!"

Roger squirmed in his seat and his face turned ashen.

Flo realized they'd grossly misunderstood. "Not *that* part, you two. Come on! Get your minds out of the gutter."

Roger's face regained some color. "Thank goodness. I'm assuming you mean his head?" His tone indicated he thought the head was less important than what he'd been thinking.

Flo nodded. She took them quickly through the fiasco in the coop and the subsequent, mini-fiasco at the stump, ending with the literal scrap of evidence she'd been able to collect.

Flo slid her phone across the table so Roger could look at it. He pulled a pair of cheaters out of his pocket and carefully perused the picture. "You know, this reminds me of something, but I can't pin it down."

TC twitched violently, turning an "I can't believe it" look on Flo. "I almost forgot." She half stood and slid her hand into the pocket of her zip-up hoodie, pulling out a piece of paper that had been folded in half and then in half again. She handed it to Flo. "I found a copy of Vlad's flyer. It was in the pocket of his coat, which was hanging over his chair." She didn't look too happy about it. "It's not a match."

Flo unfolded the sheet and smoothed it with her hands. There was no red anywhere on the page. No doubt the vampire was sensitive to using anything that reminded people of blood. "Well, that's disappointing. I was kind of hoping we could help the police arrest Vlad."

Her companions nodded.

"I guess that would have been too easy," Roger grumbled.

The waitress arrived with their salads and they fell silent as she handed them around.

"Thanks, Suzie," a familiar voice said from behind Flo.

Celia Angonetti stopped behind Flo's chair and placed a hand on her shoulder, giving it a squeeze. "I heard you had some excitement today."

"She was just telling us about finding the body," TC said in a loud whisper.

Celia shook her head. "So sad. I've worked with Nanna on a couple of committees. She's such a nice woman."

Flo nodded in agreement. "And the boys. They'll be devastated."

Celia moved around the table and slid gracefully into a chair. She used her fingers to arrange the hair in front of her ears and frowned. She'd recently had her blond bob cut into a cute pixie hairstyle that favored her delicate features and made her look like a stylish elf. "Do the police have any idea who did it?" She asked the question of Flo, which could either mean she assumed Flo would have stuck her nose into it by that point, or that she'd know because she worked a few days a month cataloging evidence down at the police station.

Either way, her assumption was correct. "Detective Peters found evidence at the scene. But I don't think they've connected it with anyone yet," Flo told her.

"I wonder if it has to do with Flavorgate."

Everyone at the table blinked in confusion. Finally, TC asked, "Flavorgate?"

Celia nodded. "The scandal about the Juicy Bird project." When they still stared at her in obvious confusion, Celia went on. "I can't believe none of you heard about this. Potts is at war with Chisholm's Chickens over some flavoring formula that Chisholm's lead scientist came up with. They were in the process of patenting the formula when the scientist suddenly left, after sabotaging the patent, and started working for Dave Potts."

Roger shook his head. "Tacky, but how much of a motive is that, really? Chicken flavoring?"

Celia shrugged. "Mass thought the formula would bring in up to a million in additional business a year for Chisolm's. For a small, family business, that's a considerable motive."

"But couldn't Chisolm's just hurry the formula to market and beat Potts at his own game?" Flo asked.

"He can't," Roger said. "I remember the case now. Chisholm has no record of the formula. The scientist who developed it did too good a job of expunging it from their database. He tried going after Potts legally, but Potts is claiming he owns the expertise for the formula because he employs the person who created it."

"That's a pretty weak argument," Flo said, frowning.

"It is," Roger agreed. "But Potts plays tennis with the judge who presided over the initial challenge. Ultimately, Chisholm would probably have won, but Potts was trying to stall the legal challenge long enough to get the first roasters with the flavor injections to market. The first one to capture market share wins."

"Nice guy," TC murmured before taking a bite of her salad.

"Yeah," Celia agreed. "According to Mass, it's kind of a miracle nobody's killed Dave Potts before this."

CHAPTER EIGHT

FLO KNOCKED ON AGNES'S door before heading back to her apartment. She'd brought her friend a slice of chocolate cream pie from *Gioppino's*, thinking it might cheer her up.

Agnes didn't answer her door. Flo was about to use her extra key when the door to the apartment next to Agnes's opened. Her friend came strolling out with her fat cat Tolstoy in her arms and a wide smile on her face.

Flo watched with interest as a big guy with sparkling brown eyes, a messy mop of dark hair, and a smile that matched Agnes's for happiness leaned against the door frame and offered her his hand.

"It was a pleasure to see you again, Agnes. And your wonderful cat too. Don't be a stranger, hear?"

The man's voice was soft and warm, with a Southern Indiana lilt that made Flo miss her birth home and what was left of her family down south.

Agnes gave a throaty giggle that made Flo's mouth drop open. They were flirting with each other! Flo's mouth continued to hang open as the door closed and Agnes did a happy little dance step.

Then she snapped it shut so she could tease her friend. "Why Agnes Willard, you old dog," she whispered loudly. "What was that all about?"

Agnes jumped and yelped in surprise. She glared at Flo. "Don't sneak up on me like that, Flo."

"I didn't sneak. I was just standing there. Is that the real reason you blew me off earlier?"

Agnes put a finger to her lips and hurried over, opening her door and pushing Flo inside. She set her cat down onto the tile inside the door and Tolstoy dropped to his wide boohind, eyeing Flo with a little too much interest for her comfort. She wagged a finger at the big cat. "Don't even think about it Grim. I'm sticking around for a long, long time."

Tolstoy yowled with disgust and trotted into the living room, where he jumped up on the windowsill and proceeded to bathe himself.

"Who is that man?" Flo asked, dropping her teasing tone. It was clear Agnes really liked the man in the apartment next door and Flo didn't want to make her feel strange about it. She was really happy for her friend.

"Hertz Thomson."

"Old Mr. Thomson's son?"

Agnes nodded. "You knew that Mr. Thomson passed a few weeks ago?"

Flo nodded.

"Well, Hertz has been cleaning out his place, and he's decided to stay there for a while. He says he really likes Silver Hills because he's met such wonderful people here." Agnes's broad face pinkened with pleasure.

"You like him, don't you?" Flo asked gently.

At first, Flo thought her friend would deny it, but she finally nodded, sighing wistfully. "I'm sure he doesn't feel the same way about me, but we've been spending a lot of time together lately. His cat Belle likes Tolstoy. They get along like a house afire." She grinned. "It's the cutest thing, Flo. You should see them play."

Flo found herself grinning, Agnes's happiness was infective. "Oh, hun. That's so wonderful. And I can tell you that man is definitely interested. It was all over his face when he looked at you."

The flush in Agnes's cheeks deepened and her eyes sparkled. "I'm not sure about that, but he seems to like me okay." She shrugged. "I'm not a very girly person." She frowned and Flo remembered Roger's insights about Agnes. He'd been spot on. She wasn't nearly as confident as she always seemed.

Flo gave her an impulsive hug. "You're an amazing person and you deserve every bit of happiness you can grab, Agnes Willard, don't you ever doubt that."

Agnes seemed more embarrassed by the sentiment than pleased and quickly changed the subject. "Is that for me?" she asked, nodding toward the Styrofoam container of pie.

"It is. TC, Roger and I went to *Gioppino's* tonight. I thought you might enjoy a snack."

Agnes started to reach for the container and then stopped. "You know what? Thanks. But I think I'm going to try to drop a few pounds. I have a doctor's appointment coming up in a few weeks. I don't want her to yell at me again."

Flo eyed her friend carefully. "That's a good plan, hun. But I hope you don't think you need to change yourself for Mr.

Thomson. If he's the right one for you, he'll accept you just the way you are."

"It's not that. It's just..." She frowned. "I want to stick around for a long time too. And I know I need to start being better about my health or that's not going to happen."

Flo hugged her again. "Like I said, you're amazing. And I should get going. See you at breakfast?"

"Yep, see you in the morning."

Flo left Agnes's place with a bounce in her step. She was so happy her friend had a romance. Even if it didn't ultimately go anywhere, it was good for Agnes to have someone care about her the way she deserved to be cared about.

She stepped off the elevator and turned toward her apartment, hearing Rodney barking stridently as soon as she started up the hallway. Alarm spiked. He rarely barked like that unless there was a stranger in or around the apartment.

And if he'd been barking for very long, her neighbors would be complaining to Vlad. The last thing Flo needed was a visit from the cranky vamp to ruin her night.

She hurried toward the door, key in hand, and jolted to a stop as a figure unfolded itself from one of the chairs in the alcove across the hall.

Her pulse spiked until she recognized the woman hurrying toward her.

Nanna Potts seemed upset. Of course, her husband had just been murdered. She would naturally be upset, but the other woman seemed more than that. She seemed terrified too.

"Oh, Mrs. Bee, I'm so glad you came back. I didn't know who else to talk to."

Rodney's barking gained a level in stridency and he flung himself at the door, his tiny nails making clacking sounds against the wood.

Flo gave Nanna a sympathetic look. "Has something else happened? You look even more upset than earlier."

Nanna nodded and shivered, her teeth clacking together. The poor woman was going to go into shock if Flo didn't do something. "Come on inside, Nanna. I'll make us some tea."

Flo grabbed Rodney up and carried him into the kitchen, giving him one of his favorite dog cookies and sending him off to gnaw happily on it.

She turned to Nanna Potts, who was rubbing her arms as if she were cold, her haunted gaze sliding around Flo's apartment but not really appearing to see it.

"Have a seat at the table," Flo told her, motioning toward the small, round table in the corner of her tiny kitchen. "You look half frozen and this is the warmest room in the house." She put a kettle on to boil and went into the living room, coming back with her favorite afghan and draping it over Nanna's shoulders.

Nanna tugged it close and shuddered. "Thank you, Flo. You're very kind to take me in like this. I didn't think I could sit in our house tonight."

Flo settled cups, sugar, and cream onto the table and draped teabags into the cups. "I can certainly understand that. Can you stay with one of the boys for a while?"

"No. They have their own lives. I don't want to impose on them." She shuddered again. "Maybe I'll go to a hotel tonight. The boys will be here in the morning. Things will be better then."

The kettle whistled happily. The sound seemed to scrape across Nanna's nerves, making her twitch and wince.

Flo handed her friend a steaming cup. "Add lots of sugar to this, hun. You look like you're about to go into shock."

Nanna nodded and complied, adding two teaspoons and stirring it thoughtfully, her sad gaze locked onto the steeping tea. "I just can't believe he's gone."

Flo patted Nanna's hand. "I know, hun. It was so sudden. You didn't have a chance to prepare."

Nanna's lips twisted. "I'm not sure how you prepare for that," she ground out, her voice filled with anger.

Flo didn't respond. She sipped her tea, waiting for the other woman to explain why she was there.

Nanna took a careful sip and closed her eyes. "That's perfect. Thank you."

"Of course. Would you like something to eat? I have a lemon poppy seed loaf." Flo glanced toward the plastic container on the counter. She frowned when she saw the vastly reduced size of the loaf. She recalled leaving Agnes in the kitchen alone the night before while she changed for yoga class. "That is unless Agnes has eaten it all."

Nanna placed a hand on her round stomach. "I couldn't eat a thing. My stomach's all twisted with nerves. But thank you."

They sipped in silence for another moment before Flo decided she was going to have to nudge Mrs. Potts into revealing her intentions. "I'm really happy to see you, of course. But you didn't come for tea, I presume?"

"No. I didn't come for tea. I came to hire you to find out who killed my husband."

Flo was surprised by the offer. "Oh. Of course. I'll help in any way I can." She tilted her head. "You know the police are very good. Detective Peters will get to the bottom of this."

Rather than easing the tension from her attractive face, Flo's words seemed to upset Nanna more. "That's just it, Flo. I'm afraid they're going to get to a false bottom and stop."

"False bottom? What do you mean?"

Nanna sighed, rubbing her eyes. "I'm afraid that, once they start looking into Dave's death, they're going to think I killed him myself."

Flo couldn't bring herself to object to that potential outcome. She knew the statistics, and she knew how cops thought. She'd spent enough time down at the Silver City Police Department, listening to the officers talk about open cases and asking questions. But she hadn't just been blowing smoke when she told Nanna that Detective Peters was good.

He had a giant stick firmly lodged in his behind, but he was a good cop.

"Why do you think they'll suspect you?" Flo clutched her teacup, her hands going cold. "*Did* you kill him, Nanna?"

To her credit, the other woman seemed to expect the question. "I did not, Flo." She laughed, but there was no humor in the sound. "I had my moments when I would have liked to pinch his head off." She blanched, seeming to realize how that sounded, given the circumstances. But she shook it off. "I had nothing to do with his murder. I loved him, Mrs. Bee. In spite of everything."

Flo believed her. She embraced a sense of relief, nodding. "Good. Then I'll be happy to help you find the killer. But I'll need you to be brutally honest with me, Nanna. Do you have any idea who killed your husband?"

Nanna ran a fingertip around the edge of her teacup, frowning.

"Nanna?"

She sighed. "Yes. I think it was the woman he was sleeping with. The one he was getting ready to leave me for."

CHAPTER NINE

FLO SAT IN SILENCE for a beat, taken by surprise. Her first thought was that it was no wonder Nanna believed Detective Peters would look at her as a suspect. Her second thought was to wonder if she'd made a mistake promising to help the other woman. "Are you sure he was having an affair?"

Nanna's eyes filled with tears. "I wish I wasn't. But, yes. He all but admitted it to me."

"He told you?"

"Not in so many words, but I accused him and he didn't deny it. He just told me to trust him, he knew what he was doing." She laughed meanly. "I might have said something cruel to him at that point. If he knew what he was doing in the bedroom, he must have learned it very recently." She pressed her knuckles against her lips, the tears slipping down her cheeks. "I was snarky with him. And they were the last words I ever spoke to my husband."

Flo blinked. "Wait, you had this conversation right before Mr. Potts went back to the coop? Just before he was..."

"Killed. Yes." She shook her head. "I keep thinking if I hadn't been so cruel, maybe he'd have stayed at the house with me. But when he was upset or needed to think something through, he always retreated to that place. He said it calmed him to fuss with the birds and do small repairs."

"He was upset about your fight?" Flo asked gently.

Nanna frowned. "I'm not sure. You'd think the potential end of our marriage would upset him, wouldn't you? But he seemed almost too distracted to focus on me. He'd been on another planet lately, as if he had something worrying on his mind."

"The campaign, maybe? Was he worried about losing?"

Nanna blew air through her lips. "Oh no. He figured he had that in the bag. He has friends in the State government who were going to use their influence to help him. And that horrible man he's—he *was* running against..." Nanna seemed to have no words to describe Vlad.

Flo knew how she felt. "If he expected to win the election, what did he intend to do about his business?"

She shrugged. "He'd been trying to talk Pet into coming home and taking over for him. Just for a couple of years. But he'd already said that he'd manage the business himself if Pet wouldn't cooperate." She made a face. "Our sons want nothing to do with the chicken business, Mrs. Bee. I told Dave that but he didn't want to hear it, so he blew me off. He did that a lot. The man wore a Teflon suit where bad news was involved. It slid right off him. He chose to create his own reality."

"Tell me about this woman. Have you met her?"

"No. But I've seen her. Dave didn't know it, but I had. I followed him one night and saw him talking to her. They seemed very chummy."

"But they could just be friends," Flo tried. She just couldn't picture David Potts having an affair. He'd been a big bear of a man, hairy and coarse looking. She'd always thought Nanna was too good for him. But another woman...

"They embraced, Ms. Bee."

Flo stared at her tea, unwilling to look at the pain in the other woman's eyes. "I'm so sorry."

Nanna shrugged. "I'll come to terms with it. But only after I know she's in jail for killing him."

"Why do you think it was her?"

"It was her. I'm sure of it." Nanna's pretty face was formed into a belligerent mask. She was determined to believe the other woman killed her husband. Flo could understand the appeal of seeing the woman who was about to destroy her life go to prison. But if Flo was going to find the killer, she needed facts and reality. Jealousy wasn't a good enough reason to focus on Dave Potts's mistress. "Do you have any idea who she is? Where would I find her?"

Nanna blinked at Flo for a beat. "Well yes. I'm sorry, I thought you knew about the scandal."

"Scandal?"

"Yes. That scientist who left Chisholm's Chickens to work for Dave."

"I had heard about that," Flo said, nodding. "But what does it have to do with..." She suddenly realized what Nanna was telling her. "The scientist is the other woman?"

"Yes. Blast her eyes. Nobody could understand why she'd leave Chisholm's. She was treated very well there by all accounts. Paid exceptionally well too. But she suddenly left it all behind and came to work at Potts Farms, just like that. Nobody understood," Nanna said angrily. "But I understand. She'd succumbed to the Potts charm. Dave oozed charm. Simply oozed it."

Flo barely kept from grimacing. Charm wasn't what Flo believed David Potts oozed, but she pressed her lips together. "You believe this woman gave up money and security for romance?" She hadn't meant to, but her tone was colored by disbelief. Flo just couldn't see it.

"I know you're skeptical, Mrs. Bee. I don't blame you. Unless you've spent time with Dave, been pulled into his sphere, you wouldn't understand how charming he could be. He could also be a hard man—brusque and seemingly cold at times. But I knew the real Dave. And I know how captivating he could be."

Flo would have to take the woman's word on that. She gave Nanna's hand a squeeze. "I'll look into it, hun. See what I can find. I'll need to talk to this woman so I'd appreciate it if you don't speak to her. I don't want to scare her off."

Nanna nodded. "I'm not going near her. When the boys get here, I'm going to ask them to deal with business issues until we figure out what we're going to do with Potts Farms."

Flo stood and walked Nanna to the door. "Try not to worry about all this," she told the other woman. "Put it out of your mind and get through the next few days. Your boys will need you to be strong."

Nanna nodded, sniffled, and gave Flo an impulsive hug. "Thanks so much for helping me, Flo. I feel better having you on my side."

"That's very kind, hun. I'll be in touch, okay?" As Nanna turned to go, Flo remembered the gold chain she'd found in the coop. "Nanna, could you wait a minute? There's something I wanted to show you."

"Sure."

Flo ran into her bedroom and pulled the slacks she'd worn that afternoon from the laundry. She'd forgotten about the jewelry when she'd changed. Digging in the pocket, she pulled it out and hurried back out to the entranceway. "Do you recognize this chain?"

It was clear as soon as Nanna saw the jewelry that she did. Her eyes went wide with pleasure. "You found my necklace. Where was it?"

"It was—um—in the supply room of the chicken coop. I found it in a corner. Behind the shovel." Flo watched the other woman carefully for her reaction to the news.

Nanna frowned. She held it up and looked at it, examining the broken clasp. "I must have lost it when I went to feed the chickens." She shook her head, smiling. "Thank you for returning it to me. David gave me this for my birthday. I was devastated when I lost it."

Flo considered taking it back from Nanna and giving it to Detective Peters as she'd intended. But there was really no apparent connection to the murder, and the jewelry seemed to have sentimental value. "You're welcome, hun. Have a good night."

Nanna nodded and left, scraping tears from her cheeks as she started toward the elevator.

Something warm bumped up against her leg and Flo looked down, finding Rodney standing there with a drooping tail and glassy eyes. He didn't bark at Nanna or even seem willing to pitch the tiniest fit over having a visitor.

Instead, he lay down on the floor and put his head on his paws, giving a shaky sigh.

Alarm spiraled through Flo at the sight. She bent down and ran her hand along the little dog's form. He didn't even look up.

He was quivering and felt warmer than usual. Flo hurriedly scooped him up. She walked back inside and closed the door, her foot squelching down on something on the floor. She looked down and saw a pile of vomit. "Oh noes, little man." She kissed his soft head. "You're not feeling well at all, are you? I guess I'm taking you to the vet tomorrow, aren't I?"

Flo didn't like how listless the little dog was. She realized he was too sick to wait until the following day to see the vet. They'd have to make a special trip to the emergency clinic.

Rodney's long form convulsed and stiffened and he vomited again. Flo barely got her shoes out of the way in time.

She couldn't wait. She needed to get him to that clinic. Flo briefly considered calling Roger to ask him to drive her so she could hold Rodney, but it was late and she hated to drag him out of his cozy apartment just to drive fifteen minutes to the clinic.

She could manage it herself.

With that bracing thought, Flo grabbed her purse and headed out of the apartment, her miserable little dog clutched in her arms.

By the time they arrived at the clinic, Rodney had begun to groan in pain. She hurried in and the two young women behind the long counter looked up and gave her a weary smile. "Hello. What can we do to help?"

"My dog is really sick. I think he's throwing up blood." And Flo had the evidence on her knee to prove it. The Dachshund had thrown up two more times on the way to the clinic.

The women jerked quickly into motion. One of them came around the counter and took Rodney. "I'll get him settled and the doctor will look him over. By the time you're done with your paperwork, the doctor will be ready to see you."

Flo nodded, her gaze following them away as a feeling of dread tightened in her belly.

"Here you go, ma'am," the girl behind the counter said, handing her an intimidating pile of paper. "I just need you to fill these out for us."

THEY PUT HER IN AN examination room and left her. Flo was really starting to be concerned by the time the veterinarian finally came into the room. The woman was carrying a clipboard and wore a frown on her plain face.

She looked to be in her mid-thirties, with long, stringy dark hair that split around oversized ears and sat limply on narrow shoulders. Her white lab coat was discolored, looking like it had been washed about a hundred times too many, and no longer fit around her middle.

She gave Flo a nod. "Mrs. Bee."

Flo jumped out of the chair she'd been perched in, her nerves jangling. "Is he all right?" Even as she asked the question, tears flooded from her eyes and Flo saw stars. If she didn't calm down soon, she was going to have a stroke.

"He's stable, but I won't lie to you. He's one sick little boy."

Flo twined her hands together and tried to keep breathing through the panic. "Is he—will he make it?"

The vet's frown deepened. "The next few hours are key. If we can get him through the night, I think he'll be all right. But he's going to have to stay here for a couple of days for observation."

"What's wrong with him?" Flo asked.

"Pancreatitis. It's a good thing you brought him right in tonight, Mrs. Bee. If you hadn't..." She shook her head, her expression dire. "Has he gotten into the trash lately, Mrs. Bee? Or did you feed him something really fatty like butter or gravy?"

Flo's eyes went wide. "No, of course not. I'm very strict about what he eats. He gets his kibble and the occasional dog cookie."

"What brand of dog food and cookie?"

Flo told her, her fingers twining more quickly as she realized how close she'd come to losing her dog that night. "He shouldn't have gotten sick from those, right?"

"Unlikely."

"Then what happened? Why is he so sick?"

"Sometimes older dogs get pancreatitis unrelated to food, drugs or any external cause. The good news is that his case is serious but probably not life-threatening. We'll keep him on IV fluids tonight and see how he is tomorrow. If the symptoms have settled down enough for him to go home, we'll send special food and antibiotics along with him."

Flo took a deep breath, relief flooding her. "Okay, that sounds good. Thank you for taking such good care of my boy."

The vet finally smiled. "It's my pleasure. He seems like a sweet old guy."

Flo laughed. "Clearly you're not seeing him at his best. If he gets to feeling better tomorrow, you might want to look alive before putting your fingers anywhere near his mouth."

The vet's lips twitched. "Noted. I'll call you in the morning to tell you how he is. Is there anything else you need from us?"

"No. Thank you so much."

Flo left the clinic a half hour later, dazed at the cost of the care Rodney was going to need and feeling sad and lonely. An angry-looking young man held the door for her and she thanked him absently, barely glancing at him as she stepped into a misty rain outside.

She wasn't sure she was going to be able to sleep without her little boy next to her. She'd come to depend on his nasal snores and stubby little legs poking her in the side all night.

Flo laughed to herself, clicking the remote to open her car door. How pathetic was she that she needed to be aurally and physically pummeled before she could sleep?

CHAPTER TEN

"THERE SHE IS."

Flo waved to the table of her friends in the dining room. Roger stood and pulled out her chair as she approached, leaning in to kiss her cheek.

"We were getting worried about you, doll. Are you feeling all right?"

"Yeah, Flo," Agnes said around a mouthful of toast. "I never beat you down to breakfatht." The last word was emphasized by wet, flying crumbs, one of which landed next to Flo's plate.

She glared at Agnes and patted Roger's hand. "I'm fine. I just got to bed late. I'm afraid I overslept."

She lowered herself into her chair and looked up as Becky, Flo's favorite waitress, hurried over with a steaming pot of coffee.

"Coffee, Mrs. Bee?"

"Please. I'll just have some oatmeal this morning, hun."

"You got it. Would you like raisins in yours too?"

Flo felt her eyes go wide. "Raisins? Ish. No thanks." She cocked her head at the young girl. "Why do you ask? I hate raisins, you know that."

Becky slid a grin toward Agnes, who was busily trying to eat around a wrinkled black lump in her spoon. "It appears things are changing."

Agnes grimaced, dropping her spoon into the bowl with disgust. "Raisins are still Satan's boogers."

"Why on earth are you having them in your oatmeal then, fool?"

"I'm trying to eat healthy, Flo. I told you that."

Flo eyed the small pile of slimy raisins in the bottom of Agnes's bowl. "Did you actually eat any of them?"

Agnes's lip curled. "Heck no!"

Roger chuckled, shaking his head.

"Then what's the point?" Flo asked quite reasonably.

Shrugging, Agnes poked at the ugly fruit with her spoon. "I was thinking maybe some of the vitamins in them would leach out into the oatmeal, then I could get the benefits without actually eating the nasty things."

"Raisins are actually not that good for you, Agnes," Roger told her. "Dried fruit is full of sugar."

Agnes's face split into a wide grin. "I knew I liked you, Roger Attles."

He chuckled. "Why don't you just have Becky put some apples and nuts into it. You'd get far more benefit. Or even a banana."

Agnes pounded the table with her fist, causing Old Mrs. Peoples at the next table to snort awake and glare in her direction.

"Do you mind, whippersnapper?" the cranky nonagenarian hissed. "Some of us are trying to have a relaxing breakfast."

Agnes gave her a wave. "Sorry. Go on back to your nap. *You old grump*," Agnes mumbled. "By the way, if you got any more relaxed you'd be drooling into your breakfast."

Old Mrs. Peoples stuck her tongue out at Agnes.

Becky bounced over and placed a bowl of oatmeal in front of Flo, along with a pitcher of cream and some brown sugar.

"Thanks, hun. I'm sorry to throw you off schedule today," Flo said.

"Oh, you're fine, Mrs. Bee. But I heard that you came in late last night. Is everything okay?"

Flo sighed. "Not entirely. Rodney took sick. He's at the emergency clinic on the East end of town."

"Oh no," Roger said, his handsome face folding into a frown. "I'm so sorry, doll. Why didn't you wake me?"

She shook her head. "There was no sense in both of us losing sleep."

"No wonder you overslept," Agnes said. "Is he going to be okay?" Despite the fact that Agnes and Rodney had a long-running feud, with animus on both sides, she seemed genuinely upset to hear that the little dog was ill.

Flo nodded. "I think so. The vet called before I came down and said he was resting comfortably and seemed to be feeling better." Flo frowned. "She wants to keep him another day or two though. She said he's dehydrated."

"Poor old guy," Roger said, squeezing her hand. "He'll be right as rain soon, doll. You'll see."

She nodded, hoping he was right. "Well, I'm going to keep myself busy so I don't worry." She glanced at Agnes. "Feel like a visit to the police station this morning?"

"What for?" Agnes's wide face turned suspicious.

"I need to talk to someone about David Potts." Flo hoped Agnes would presume she meant one of the detectives. Unfortunately, her friend wasn't that slow on the draw.

She lifted one, bushy brown eyebrow and gave Flo a look. "*Which* someone?"

Flo sighed. "We'll bring donuts, it will be fine."

Agnes crossed her beefy arms over her chest, and her expression turned mulish. "Uh, uh. I'm not going to be date bait again, Flo. Do you have any idea what it's like to go on a date with Meanie?"

Fortunately, Flo did not. "No dates, I promise. I just need you to smile a little and ply him with donuts. It will be painless, I promise."

Flo knew she was going to regret that promise, but desperate times called for desperate measures.

"Morning!" TC bounced up to them as Flo was tucking into her oatmeal. She looked up and smiled at her young friend. "Good morning, sunshine. You look bright-eyed and bushy-tailed."

TC nodded. "I don't have any activities scheduled this morning." She dropped into Celia's chair, which was suspiciously empty. "I was wondering if you were doing any investigating today."

Roger barely hid his surprise and Agnes didn't even try. Her mouth fell open and she punched TC on the arm. "You're back?"

TC rubbed her arm, frowning. "Yeah. If you promise never to punch me again. That hurt."

Agnes cackled happily. "The Three Musketeers ride again."

"More like the Three Stooges," TC said.

Flo ate a few more bites of oatmeal and sipped her coffee. "Okay then. Let's get going, Curly and Larry. We have a Meanie to manipulate."

"I DON'T KNOW WHY YOU always get to be Mo," Agnes complained as they entered the police station.

Flo rolled her eyes as TC chuckled. "Because I'm a natural born leader."

"Naturally bossy, you mean," Agnes grumbled. "I think you should be Larry or Curly for a while. I'll be Mo."

TC raised her hand. "I'd like to go on record as not wanting to be *any* of the Three Stooges." When the two older women looked at her in surprise, she shrugged. "I prefer someone a little more contemporary and less weird."

"Contemporary?" Flo asked, slightly offended. "You mean, like Lucy Ricardo?"

"Or Carol Burnett," Agnes added."

TC's lips twitched. "Maybe even a little bit more contemporary than that. And less slap-sticky."

Agnes shook her head. "Youngsters."

TC chuckled.

"If you don't like slap-stick you really shouldn't hang out with Agnes," Flo said on a grin. She shoved the box of donuts into Agnes's stiff hands. "And about the Mo thing, you're just cranky that I wouldn't let you have a donut."

"I don't want a donut." She frowned. "Well, I do want one, but I'm determined not to have it."

TC and Flo shared a look. If Agnes was going to be cranky with her new diet changes, their lives were going to be a whole lot pricklier over the next few weeks. Flo patted her friend's beefy arm. "Let's get this done and I'll take you for a surprise."

Agnes glanced suspiciously at Flo. "A surprise? There's nothing green in this surprise, is there? Because I'm not a rabbit or a cow. That stuff you and TC always eat in a bowl for lunch is only a surprise to your poor stomachs, which are crying out for real food."

Flo shook her head. She scanned a look over the information desk at the center of the surprisingly unoccupied room. Even the wood benches along the walls were empty. "I guess crime's taking a holiday," she told her friends. "Hopefully Meanie's not taking one too."

The sound of one of those jet-powered hand drying machines blared into the quiet of the room and, a moment later, the Men's restroom door burst open and belched Meanie Meldick into the hallway. His wide form ambled toward his desk, his beefy hands tugging on the waistband of his pants to straighten them.

Flo grimaced. "Good heavens, couldn't he manage his affairs before he returned to the public area?" she murmured.

"I don't even want to think about that, let alone see it happening," TC agreed.

"Here goes nothing." Agnes stalked away from them, holding the box of donuts in front of her like an offering to the gods.

Meanie's head jerked up and his beady eyes widened at the sight of Agnes striding toward him. The quick skittering of his gaze toward Flo and TC told Flo he hadn't known he had company.

Meanie's greasy brow lowered over his small eyes. Then he spotted the bakery box and he perked up. "Hello, Agnes."

Agnes smiled at the cop, sliding the box of donuts onto the top of his desk. "How are you, Officer Meldick?"

"I think we're past the formal name thing, aren't we Agnes?" He waggled his brows suggestively.

TC made a retching sound.

Flo shushed her, walking over to the desk. "Officer Meldick."

He was already reaching for the box of donuts, his thick fingers snapping the lid back with practiced ease. "Mrs. Bee. Since you brought the lovely Agnes and the even lovelier box of donuts, I'm assuming you're here to ply me for information."

Nobody ever said the man was stupid.

"I was just wondering if there was any news on the David Potts investigation."

Meldick shoved a donut into his mouth, nodding happily as he chewed. When he'd swallowed, he winked at Agnes. "You brought my favorite kind."

Agnes leaned her arms on the surface of the raised desk, tilting toward him with a conspiratorial smile. "I did. It was easy since we share similar tastes in fine pastries."

His grin showed chewed donut behind his teeth.

Ugh!

Flo gritted her teeth and hung in there. "The investigation, Officer Meldick?"

He swallowed, settling the rest of his chocolate frosted glazed donut back into the box. "You know I can't give you information on an ongoing case, Mrs. Bee."

"Not even for me?" Agnes asked, reaching out to smooth her hand over his shoulder.

Dandruff flakes filtered off the dark blue fabric, sifting downward.

Retching noises ensued near the door.

"What did you want to know," he asked, looking dubious.

"Was there any evidence left behind?" Agnes asked him. "Any suspects?"

"You were there. You saw it. There wasn't much." Then he grinned widely. "Especially after you skated through all of it."

Agnes frowned at the reminder. She'd had to give her shirt and sneakers over to evidence collection. Peters insisted he needed to test the blood Agnes had trod through on her ungainly trip to the stump. "Don't remind me. I lost half my clothes in that small transgression."

Meldick leered at her, the caterpillars over his eyes dancing with suggestion.

Behind Flo, TC sounded as if she was about to hork up a hippo. "What about that small piece of paper I saw on the ground?" Flo asked.

Meanie's leer died a hurried death. He frowned. "You're entirely too nosy for your own good, Mrs. Bee."

"I can't help what I saw," she told him. "Do you think it came from the killer?"

He shrugged, looking sly. "It's probably nothing. We're barely looking at it."

Something in the way he said it brought up Flo's antennas. "Why not? Do you already know who killed Potts?"

Meanie shoved the donut into his mouth and stared at her while he chewed. He had no intention of voluntarily spilling whatever he knew. Flo would have to trick it out of him.

She glanced at Agnes. "I knew it was her."

Agnes nodded. "She seemed like the obvious one to kill him. I mean, knowing what we now know."

Meanie's small eyes widened.

Flo gave Meanie a look. "I guess we're done here. Enjoy your donuts, Officer Meldick."

Meldick swallowed hard. "Wait!"

Flo halted in her turn and looked expectantly at him. "Yes?"

"Who are you talking about? What do you know?"

Flo stared at him just as he'd stared at her.

It took him only a beat to catch what she was throwing. He sighed. "Okay, I'll tell you something and you tell me something. Deal?"

Flo pretended to consider it for a moment before sighing. "I hate to give you my information, it's prime stuff."

Meanie leaned closer. "Not as prime as what I have."

She shrugged. "Okay, you go first."

"No, you go first."

"You don't trust me?" Flo let amazement fill her expression.

There was a two-second standoff before Agnes stepped in. "Flo's as good as her word, Melny."

The man's expression turned dewy at the endearment.

"Argh! Oh my gosh."

Flo flapped her hand behind her back in an attempt to silence TC, who was coughing loudly behind her hand.

Meldick's gaze started to lift in TC's direction. Flo moved sideways to block his view. "Well, Officer? Do we have an accord?"

Meldick fixed her with a beady stare, but Flo waited him out. Finally, he nodded. "The ax we found at the scene..." He leaned closer, his greasy face earnest. "It belonged to Dave Potts himself."

Flo was disappointed. "That's not a very big scoop."

Meldick rolled his eyes. "That's not the scoop. The fingerprints are the scoop."

"What fingerprints?" Flo asked. She felt the warmth of another body and turned to see TC next to her. She'd been drawn to the train wreck against her will.

Meldick shook his head. "I can't give you a name. But I will tell you that the suspect knows the victim well." Meldick's caterpillar-like brows lifted with innuendo. "*Really* well."

Try as she might, Flo couldn't get Meanie to tell her anything else. He was a vault. A big, hairy, sweaty vault with donut breath.

Flo finally gave up. "Okay, thanks for your help, Officer Meldick." She started to turn toward the door, but a harshly cleared throat stopped her. She turned back to see Meldick glaring at her. "Aren't you forgetting something?"

Flo had been hoping he'd be the one to forget. No such luck. She nodded. "Of course. I'm so sorry. I just got really excited by your information." The dry look she gave him didn't even register. His expression never changed. She stepped closer, lowering her voice. "I have it on good authority that David Potts was having an affair."

Excitement lit Meldick's eyes. Clearly, Flo's information meshed with their suspicions. Which told Flo all she needed to know about their suspect.

Detective Peters believed Nanna killed her own husband.

Her client had been right. The police were playing the odds.

It was a good thing Nanna Potts had hired Flo.

CHAPTER ELEVEN

CELIA CAME RUNNING over to them when they arrived back at Silver Hills an hour later. Flo had treated Agnes to a sugar-free, fat-free, and according to Agnes, taste-free frozen yogurt at the *Slow Yo* Yogurt shop before bringing her back home.

Rather than make her friend feel better, the treat seemed to have enhanced Agnes's bad mood. She stomped inside and sent the dining room a longing glance. Or, more precisely, the door leading into the kitchen from the dining room, where the delicious scent of lunch was already wafting outward.

Fortunately, Celia's news quickly took Agnes's mind from food. Though probably not for long.

"Finally!" Celia exclaimed as she scurried toward them. "I thought you'd never get back."

"We've only been gone a couple of hours, Ce," Flo told her.

They'd tried to get into the Potts Farms offices to speak to the scientist whom Nanna had accused of carrying on an affair with her husband and then killing him. Unfortunately, the girl at the information desk hadn't been helpful at all, claiming the woman wasn't there. Flo suspected she was, but she didn't have the authority to force the issue. They'd come back to Silver Hills to regroup and consider their options.

"I have news on the election!" Celia told them in a harsh whisper. She glanced toward the office and grabbed Flo's arm, pulling her toward the empty dining room. TC and Agnes followed, obviously intrigued.

"What in the world is going on?" Flo asked her friend.

Celia grinned. "Egor's here."

She was referring to Vlad's campaign manager, whose real name nobody bothered to ask. Flo knew his name was Preston Jamison, but it was way too much fun just to call him Egor. Flo frowned. "And that's news why?"

"Because I overheard them talking. I was sitting in that chair that's kind of hidden behind the big potted palm near the stairs."

Flo nodded. She knew the one. It had gotten more than one resident in trouble when they hadn't known someone was nearby. Barney Tattle and Elisa Kemp had been caught canoodling in an alcove one evening, about an hour after dinner. And Mrs. Barney Tattle hadn't been any too pleased by the event. Most particularly because the canoodling hussy had a lock on the gossip in Silver Hills. That was when Flo had learned just what a degenerate gossip Elisa Kemp had become. She was so hooked on the practice she hadn't even been able to keep from gossiping about herself.

To make matters worse, Mrs. Tattle had somehow gotten the worst end of the scandal. Elisa had magically turned herself into a victim.

Such is the power of innuendo and carefully crafted speculation.

"Flo?"

Flo blinked. "Oh, sorry. I drifted away there for a moment."

Celia sighed. "I'm wasting this news on you. You're not paying attention."

"I'm sorry. What did you overhear?"

"Well, Egor came to tell Vlad something that put a stake in his tiny little black heart." Celia's grin widened. She was certainly relishing the news she was about to tell them.

TC laughed. "You're killing us, Celia. What did he tell Vlad?"

"Vlad is no longer the only person in the race."

Silence dropped like a bomb between them as shock set in. Finally, TC shook her head. "I can't believe it. There's only two weeks until the election. Whoever it is won't have much time."

"Actually, I think the new candidate will be just fine," Celia said, her blue gaze sparkling. "He already has an organization, money, and the backing of all the groups who supported his father."

Flo's eyes went wide. "His father? One of Dave Potts's sons is taking over for him?"

Celia clapped her hands, nearly bouncing on her feet with glee. "Isn't that just the most exquisite torture for the vamp? He's going to swallow a stake over it."

As if her glee had yanked him from the hidden environs of his lair, Vlad exited the manager's office with Egor and stood outside, talking rapidly with hands flying. He was clearly agitated. He turned a glower on Flo and Co. as Egor made a quick escape. Flo didn't flinch as he stared her down, looking as if he blamed her for the new development.

But Flo couldn't find it within herself to feel joy at the prospect. A new worry had cropped up to join the others floating around in her mind. "Which son, Celia?"

Celia's smile finally dimmed. "I don't know. Egor just said Potts's son. He didn't say which one."

It didn't really matter, Flo thought. Whichever son it was had just been elevated to chief suspect status. And that was the good news. The bad news was that he might have become the next target of a killer.

FLO HURRIED AFTER VLAD'S campaign manager, running to catch up with him as he reached to open the door of a high-end silver SUV. "Mr. Jamison?"

The man stopped with one leg inside the car and turned to her, his face a mask of hostility. "Yes?"

Flo couldn't help wondering how Vlad expected to win hearts and minds when his campaign manager appeared to be just as unfriendly as he was. Despite the unwelcoming glower, Flo smiled and offered him her hand. "We haven't formally met. I'm Florence Bee."

Actually, Vlad had introduced Flo and Co. to his campaign manager once, but Flo had been so shell-shocked at the time she hadn't returned the introduction. And Preston Jamison hadn't seemed the least bit interested in them.

The manager pursed his lips with disdain. "I know who you are."

Her smile tightened but held. "Let me guess, Vlad told you all about me?"

The man's mean-looking gray gaze narrowed. "Something like that."

Preston Jamison looked to be just under six feet tall, with a wide mouth and a slightly-too-large nose sporting enormous pores. A small raised scar, about half an inch long, ran from the right-hand corner of his mouth, etching his cheek. As always, he was dressed in an expensive looking dark gray suit with a pristine white shirt. However, the usual burgundy tie with tiny polka dots was missing.

Everything in his demeanor, from the tight look of un-friendliness on his plain face to the rigid way he held himself, told Flo that Vlad had already turned the man into an enemy.

She'd really been hoping he could be an ally.

"Look, Mr. Jamison. It's no secret that Vlad and I don't get along. But I can assure you I'm not necessarily an adversary to your cause." She wasn't necessarily a friend either. The jury was still out. As much as she'd love to get rid of Vlad at Silver Hills, the idea of him as Silver City's mayor was terrifying. "And I have no reason to want him to be blamed for a murder he didn't commit."

Jamison's glower darkened. "There's absolutely no evidence to prove Mr. Newsome killed that man."

"No. There isn't. You're right. But rumors will fly. Vlad was the only one who appeared to gain from David Potts's death."

"When the facts come out, there will be more suspects," Jamison said with a little too much confidence.

Flo allowed an eyebrow to arch. "Oh? Do you know some-thing I don't, Mr. Jamison?"

The man tensed visibly. After a moment, he seemed to force himself to relax, and he even gave Flo a tight smile. "Mrs. Bee, you're connected pretty closely with the rumor mills here at Silver Hills, aren't you?"

"You could say that, I guess. It's not hard to be. The rumors tend to find me, I don't go looking for them." Flo frowned, thinking of Elisa hurrying up to her just that morning with the newest gossip. "I know Vlad Newsome is your boss," she said, carefully, "but you have to know he isn't popular at Silver Hills. He could use me as an ally."

Flo let that hang there for a moment and watched the realization that she was right settle into the man's expression. He sighed, shoving his hands into the pockets of his well-fitting slacks. "You're right. I owe you an apology. I let Mr. Newsome's opinion of you color my own. I don't usually fall into that trap."

"It's okay, Mr. Jamison. Shall we start over?"

He offered her his hand. "It's a pleasure to meet you, Mrs. Bee."

She took the offering, pumping it in a firm grip that she hoped told him she was no weak-willed little old lady. "Call me Flo, please. I wanted you to know that I'm working for the widow. We're trying to discover who actually killed Dave Potts."

His brows peaked in surprise. "You have any idea who it is?"

"Not yet. But, despite my differences with Vlad, I don't want to believe it was him."

"I can assure you it wasn't."

Flo gave him a non-committal smile.

"You'll keep me apprised of your investigation?"

"No."

He blinked in surprise. "Oh."

"I just wanted to let you know I was working on it. And to ask you about the new development in the campaign."

"What new development?" He looked genuinely perplexed. He was a very good liar.

"The new candidate for mayor?"

"What? I hadn't..." his voice trailed off and he threw a glance toward the residence behind Flo.

"There's no point pretending you didn't know. Someone heard you talking to Vlad about it."

Jamison shook his head, scrubbing a hand over his face. "He hasn't announced yet. So far it's just rumor."

"The rumor mill around here isn't only fast, it's generally pretty accurate. Most of the people in Silver City are related to someone at Silver Hills. It's a small community."

Flo thought she'd heard that Jamison wasn't from Silver City. She was pretty sure he wasn't even from Indiana. Judging by the slight accent and the brusque demeanor, she guessed he hailed from New York City. "Word is the newcomer is one of the Potts boys."

Jamison didn't look happy about it. Flo had no doubt he knew what that would mean. "If that's true he'll be able to hit the ground running," she told the campaign manager. "And he'll be an instant favorite. He's young, handsome, and will have the sympathy vote on his side."

Jamison frowned down at her. "Don't sound so gleeful, Mrs. Bee."

"Not gleeful, Mr. Jamison. But I wanted you to know what you'd be up against. Also..." She took care to neutralize her tone. "If Dave Potts's death was tied to the campaign, then whoever killed the father might be gunning for the son next."

She leaned close, her gaze locked onto his. "I'm going to be watching that very closely."

She could feel his gaze on her back as she turned and walked back into Silver Hills. Flo's stomach twisted with nerves. She'd basically just told Jamison she'd be watching him and his horrible client. If Vlad or Jamison had something to do with Dave Potts's death, she had just put herself right into their crosshairs.

It was terrifying. But Flo would never forgive herself if that young boy was killed because she'd done nothing to head it off.

CHAPTER TWELVE

FLO DIALED NANNA POTTS and waited while the phone rang. She was about to disconnect when Nanna answered, her voice breathless. "Hello?"

"Hi, Nan. It's Flo Bee. How are you doing?"

The other woman took a deep breath, and Flo heard the sound of keys hitting a hard surface. "I'm okay. The boys are here. We just came back from the grocery."

"I'm glad your kids are there. A family should be together at a time like this."

"Yes. It's been good for us to be together. They've had questions, and it's helped me to talk about everything."

"Everything?" Flo frowned. She hoped Nan hadn't dropped their father's affair into the boys' laps. That was the last thing they needed to be dealing with at the moment.

"Everything they needed to know," Nan qualified in a careful tone. Flo realized one or both of the boys must be there with her.

"I wondered if I could come out to the house? I'd like to talk to you about some developments in the case."

"Of course. Can you give me a couple of hours? We were going to run to the funeral home with Dave's suit and iron out some details."

"Two hours then. I look forward to seeing the boys again. I haven't seen them for a few years. They've probably changed a lot."

The other woman chuckled warmly. "You won't recognize them. I'll see you in a couple of hours."

Flo disconnected as a knock sounded on her door. She opened it to find a man she didn't know standing in the hall. She instinctively turned, expecting Rodney to tear, barking down the hallway to accost the stranger. Then she remembered her little protector wasn't there.

A deep sadness filled her at the thought.

"Hello," Flo said tentatively. "Can I help you?"

The man smiled, offering her his hand. "We haven't met, Mrs. Bee. But I wanted to introduce myself. My father spoke very highly of you."

She shook his hand, finding it warm and slightly moist. For a beat, Flo wondered if she was looking at one of Dave Potts's sons. If so, the boys had *really* changed.

Then she realized the man standing at her door was probably three decades too old to be a Potts boy. Though there wasn't a lot of gray in his dark hair and his boyish face was virtually unlined. "Your father?"

He dropped her hand. "Anton Thomas."

Then it clicked where she'd seen him before. "You're Hertz Thomas. Agnes's friend."

His round cheeks turned pink and he looked down at the floor. "I do consider Agnes a friend. She's such a nice person."

Oh boy, Flo thought. He had it bad. She fought the grin that tried to split her face. "Agnes mentioned you'd been spending time together. She's enjoying your company." Flo hoped she wasn't laying it on too thick. The last thing she wanted to do was scare Agnes's potential beau away. But Hertz didn't look unhappy about Flo's revelation. "I enjoy her company too, Mrs. Bee. In fact, that's why I came by. I was wondering..."

Flo waited while he struggled with whatever question he wanted to ask. She couldn't shake the feeling that, if she pushed him at all, he might run away.

Finally, he took a deep breath. "I'm sorry. I'm just a little nervous."

"There's nothing to be nervous about, hun. Just spit it out. I promise I won't bite." She smiled to take the sting out of the words. Flo had things to do and, as nice as Hertz Thomas might be, she needed to get a move on.

"I was wondering..."

"You said that already, hun."

"I, um."

Flo suddenly couldn't take it anymore. "Yes, Agnes would like to go out with you. She loves going to restaurants and movies. Whatever you do, don't take her to the Roller Dome or dancing. At least not unless you have body armor and steel toed shoes."

He stood there with his mouth hanging open. For one terrified moment, Flo was afraid she'd misread his signals. But then he grinned. "Oh, thank goodness. I hate skating anyway, and I love to eat. There's a mystery movie starring cats. I was thinking maybe I'd take her to that."

"She'd love it," Flo couldn't resist reaching out to clasp his hand. "That's a perfect and very thoughtful choice, Hertz."

He flushed with embarrassment. "Okay. Good. Well, I should be going."

"Have fun at the movie, hun."

He nodded and hurried away down the hall, a definite bounce in his step.

Flo grinned after him. She really liked Agnes's new beau. And she had a feeling the two of them would get on well together.

Then she remembered Nanna and the boys. Her grin slid away. She turned back inside to grab her purse. She'd stop by the emergency clinic and see Rodney before heading out to the Potts home.

She was hoping to verify that one of the boys was running, determine which one, talk to him about his plans, warn him of the potential for danger, and see if Nan could help her get in to see the woman Dave Potts had been having an affair with.

It was a very long list.

Especially when Flo reminded herself that she needed to find a way to remove the boys from the suspect list while she was at it.

FLO DIDN'T CALL AGNES to come with her. She was afraid she'd interfere with Hertz's invitation. And to be honest, she wasn't looking forward to dealing with Miss Cranky Pants again. Maybe, once Agnes and Hertz were officially an item, Agnes would be too in love to fret about her diet overmuch.

Flo could only hope.

She knocked on TC's office door on the way out of the building, and her friend called out for her to come inside. TC looked up from a stack of paperwork, her expression a little harried.

"Hey, hun. I'm going to talk to the Potts boys in a couple of hours. I wondered if you wanted to come with?"

TC frowned. "I'd love to come. But I have too much work. And we have bowling later. You didn't forget, did you?"

Flo *had* forgotten. TC had started a once a month, inter-residence bowling league. Their first competition was that night at six. "Of course not. I'll be there with bells on."

TC didn't smile. "I don't care if you wear bells. I just need you to bring your 'A' game. You're competing against the best team on the singles side tonight."

Flo grimaced. The singles side of Silver Hills was mostly people who were in their forties and younger. Aside from having an edge on the seniors with age and strength, the Eagles had been bowling together for a couple of years. Flo had heard they were very good.

"We still have *you* though, right?"

TC frowned. "About that. One of their regulars couldn't play tonight, so I'm filling in for her. You have Roger and Celia."

Flo felt a twinge of excitement. Roger and Ce were both great bowlers.

"And Agnes."

Excitement crashed into a pool of despair. Flo had managed to cleanse that little factoid from her brain.

TC grabbed her cell phone. "I'd better call and remind the Eagles."

"Make sure you call Agnes too. She could be getting another offer for tonight. She might get so thrilled she'll forget."

TC's slender, dark brown eyebrows lifted. "Do tell." Then she flapped a hand. "Scratch that. I don't have time right now. But I insist you tell me later, over a glass of bad wine at the *Bounce and Bowl*."

Flo headed out of the residence. TC's reminder about bowling made Flo realize she hadn't gotten out to buy bowling shoes yet. She had no intention of trying to fit her extra narrow size six feet into a sweaty pair of used shoes at the bowling alley. She'd meant to get out and do it the day before, but it had totally slipped her mind with the murder and everything.

She'd have to cut her visit with Rodney short and run over to the sporting goods store.

Sighing as her list continued to grow, Flo hurried across the parking lot.

Her silver sedan was parked at the outside edge of the lot as usual. Flo liked to walk to and from her car for a little extra exercise.

But that was where *usual* stopped and *horrible* began.

When she came within a dozen feet of her car her feet suddenly stopped. Her pulse shot into the danger zone and Flo saw stars.

Someone had vandalized her car. She had a flat tire. Actually four flat tires, she noted as she moved closer and examined the damage. And the tires weren't just flat.

They'd been slashed. Brutally and with definite malice.

RICHARD AND ROGER ATTLES stood with their hands on their hips and matching frowns on their faces. Flo glanced at her watch and tried not to be impatient. "Can you fix them?"

Roger shook his head. "Sorry, doll. These are beyond fixing." He turned to his son, Richard, who was also the day manager at Silver Hills. "Do you have somebody you can call? My tire guy retired last year."

Richard nodded, sliding an apologetic glance Flo's way. "You'll have to buy four new tires, Mrs. Bee. I'm sorry." He truly looked sorry, though Flo knew he couldn't have had anything to do with the slashing.

"It's not your fault, hun. But we might want to look at adding a security guard to watch the lot."

Richard sighed. "There's no money for that, I'm afraid. But I've been looking at exterior cameras. I'm definitely going to move forward on that idea. I just wish I hadn't let Vlad talk me out of doing it already."

Flo arched a brow. "Vlad doesn't want security for the lot? What? He's afraid you'll catch him draining a villager?"

Richard chuckled. "I'm glad you've managed to retain your sense of humor, anyway."

She grimaced. "Who says I'm kidding?"

"Can I give you a ride somewhere, doll?"

"You can't, Dad," Richard told him. "You promised you'd come to Lizza's recital this afternoon."

Roger glanced at his watch. "I have time. I don't have to be there for..."

"It's in an hour," Richard reminded him.

Flo thought Lizza must be Richard's high-school-aged daughter. He didn't talk about his family much. Flo thought he was divorced. But she knew he was very proud of his only child. She was rumored to be a very talented pianist who had her eye on playing professionally someday.

"I'm sorry, doll. I promised her I'd be there. It's her last recital of the season."

"Don't give it a moment's thought," Flo reassured him. "Family comes first."

"I can call you a taxi," Richard said helpfully.

Flo was about to agree when a familiar voice hailed her from the front door. She turned as Celia and Agnes came out, waving in her direction.

When Agnes saw Flo, her dour expression lightened considerably. But then she saw Flo's tires and horror replaced the dread Flo had seen there.

Flo suspected she knew what Agnes had been dreading. "Hi ladies. Where are you off to?"

"Celia's taking me to the sporting goods store," Agnes grumbled. She eyed Flo's car with lost hope. "I wouldn't bother her, but there was *nobody* else around with a car." She eyed Flo with despair.

Flo felt her pain. "What about TC? Didn't she drive today?"

"Her car's in the shop," Richard told them. "According to TC, it's going to be there for days."

"It's no bother, really," Ce told them happily. "I was going out anyway. I need to stop by the restaurant and help Mass with the books."

Massimo Angonetti was Celia's husband and co-owner of *Gioppino's*. In Flo's opinion, the two of them had a strange marriage. They lived in separate homes, but they seemed happy and appeared to really enjoy each other's' company otherwise.

"Perfect!" Roger said happily.

Too late, Flo realized what he was about to do. The last thing she wanted was to get into a car with Celia. The woman was a frustrated Indy Car racer with zero concept of her own mortality.

Flo raised a hand to stop him, but he bowled her right over. "You can give Florence a ride. As you can see, vandals did a real number on her tires."

Ce gasped. "Oh my goodness. Honey, are you okay?"

"I'm fine. But you don't need to drag me around."

"Nonsense! There's plenty of room in my big old car. I'd love the extra company. It will be fun."

"Yeah, fun, Agnes grumbled."

Flo quickly said, "shotgun!"

"Uh, uh, Flo. You got shotgun last time. You know I get car sick in the back seat. Especially when I'm flying around, pinging off everything."

Roger's smile dimmed. "Young lady, did you have your seat belt on?"

Agnes blew a raspberry. "There was no time. Ce achieved lift-off almost before I got both feet in the car."

Celia laughed gaily. "You're so funny, Agnes."

Agnes arched a brow at Roger, making it crystal clear she wasn't joking.

"Oh, my. Maybe I can give you ladies a ride instead."

"Dad..." Richard warned.

"Don't be silly, Roger. Celia can give me a ride. You go enjoy Lizza's concert. I want a full report on it later, at bowling." Flo couldn't let Roger disappoint his family for her. She would pull on her big girl pants and strap in. After all, how bad could it be?

CHAPTER THIRTEEN

THEY TOOK THE TURN onto Main street on one point zero five wheels, sending up a squeal that had people jumping further away from the curb and staring after them with horrified expressions. Celia's big SUV roared past a small tree planted in the grassy space between the street and the sidewalk, shearing off a branch as cleanly as a chain saw with freshly sharpened blades.

Flo gasped as an elderly man moved down from the curb at the intersection and took a wobbly step into the walkway.

"Ce!"

"I see him," she said with unnatural calm. But rather than slowing to a stop, she gunned it and swerved around him at the last minute, whacking his old guy hat right off his head with the sapling branch sticking from the side mirror and sending the hat flying down the street.

All around them horns blared. Ce was oblivious to them, one and all. She barreled forward, stopped by nothing short of full red in the stop lights, and then only because the crosswalk was dense with people and she had no room to swerve around them.

Celia's tires screeched as she braked to a stop and her slender fingers drummed impatiently against the steering wheel.

Flo looked toward the passenger seat and saw only the rounded hump of Agnes's back. "Agnes? Are you all right?"

The hump moved, but Agnes's head didn't appear. She'd put herself into the crash position and Flo doubted anything she could say would pull her out of it.

Though Flo had no intention of trying to get Agnes to straighten in the seat. Her position might be the only thing that saved her when they crashed in a deadly rolling fireball.

Flo only hoped there were no innocents involved in the crash. Aside from her and Agnes, of course. They were the sacrificial lambs on the altar of Celia's denial of mortality.

Flo tried to peel her hands off the ceiling and door frame, but they didn't want to come. She'd pressure fused them to the fine black leather. Her knees were killing her from being smashed into the door frame, and she was pretty sure she'd broken one heel trying to keep from being catapulted on that last turn.

"Don't you love my new car?" Celia asked, oblivious.

"I'm not sure," Flo told her in a terror-squeezed voice. "It's hard to see it through all the flailing and flinging. Don't you want to keep it in one piece for a while longer?"

Ce laughed gaily, apparently considering Flo's question rhetorical. "You don't mind if I get a car wash before we go to the store, do you?"

Flo opened her mouth to respond just as the light changed. Ce gunned it, coming off her mark like Mario Andretti and leaving behind half the rubber of her tires as she shot away from

a dead stop to something that had to be in the high double dig-
its.

Flo couldn't look at the speedometer. She was too busy
spreading herself across the available space like a throwing star
to keep from being flung around the wide back seat.

Scenery flashed by. Flo's only impression of people on the
street was the flash of terrified eyes and the horrified "oh" of
slack lips as pedestrians leaped out of Ce's path.

The car wash was coming up fast on their left. Flo watched
the two blocks dissolve away and thought maybe Celia had forgotten she wanted to turn.

Silly Flo.

At the last possible second, Celia threw on the brakes and
spun the steering wheel, taking the turn more sideways than
forward, and came out of the skid with another blow to the gas
pedal, surging toward the line of cars waiting for the automat-
ed car wash.

Flo sincerely believed that she was living through the last
seconds of her life. She briefly lamented the coming deaths of
all the innocents waiting in line and wished she had time to
warn them.

But Celia suddenly swerved to the right and flew past the
barrier into the Frequent Washer line, barreling through on the
bumper of a big white pickup truck and cutting off the car that
was making its way through in the next lane.

Horns blared all around them.

Flo wished the horns mattered. But she'd learned all too
quickly that they had no effect on Celia Andretti—erm—Angonetti.

Flo gave a little chirp of alarm as the driveway leading to the wash took a sharp curve. The SUV skidded around the curve, barely scraping past a concrete guidepost. The force of the backwash nearly blew the blank-eyed stuffed rabbit perched on top of the barrier right off its perch, its gaily waving hand whipping the air as if it was riding a bucking bronco in the rodeo.

Flo yelped as Ce barreled up behind the white truck, hardly slowing as she approached the track into the car wash.

The driver of the truck hit the track and, no doubt seeing Ce approaching at hyper speed, gunned it and nearly ran over the young girl with the soapy water sprayer clutched in her hands. He fed the tires several feet onto the track before stopping with a jolt, no doubt to keep from hitting the car in front of him, and then oozed slowly into the soap and water jungle, disappearing safely from sight.

To her immense credit, even seeing Ce charging toward her, seemingly out of control, the young spray girl gave an admirable attempt at trying to guide Ce into the tracks. She signaled for Ce to veer right and when she was ignored, flapped her arms a bit frantically, horror writ large on her young face as the big car came right at her.

The SUV hit the track and slammed over it, heading straight for the spray girl.

She leaped out of the way at the last moment, sprayer flying into the air and coming down to smack against the windshield on Agnes's side.

The hump in the passenger seat gave a violent jerk at the sound and then dipped lower as Agnes no doubt doubled completely over in preparation for the fiery crash.

Ce laughed gaily and wrenched the wheel to the right, forcing the big vehicle's tires back over the track and then, with a final loud thump and a wrenching shudder, the car fell into the track and Ce put it into neutral, the car already entering the soaping stage.

"That was fun," she chirped gaily.

Beside her in the front seat, the sound of The Lord's Prayer emerged from the hump.

Flo hadn't even known Agnes was religious.

Flo didn't move for a long moment, letting the technicolor embrace of the scrubbing jungle wrap itself protectively around her and soothe her with its delicious slowness.

Then she forced herself to straighten in the seat and groaned as pain sheered through her entire body. She figured she'd done the equivalent of two hours of yoga with all the pushing and clenching. Her jaw hurt, and she wondered if she'd fractured a tooth or five gritting her teeth through the maneuvers.

"Oh darn it!" Ce blurted.

Flo looked up as Agnes unfurled, her head finally coming above the seat. "What's wrong?" Agnes asked. "Is there an inconvenient body stuck underneath the car? Did you run up on top of another car? Are you regretting that you had to use one tire too many on that last turn?"

Flo knew that tone of voice. Agnes was on edge. "Agnes, we're okay."

Agnes's head whipped around, her lip curled in a growl. "Don't!"

Flo pressed her lips together. She'd like to save Celia from the coming storm, but she realized she didn't have the ammunition she needed for the task.

Maybe if she had a pie to distract Agnes with.

"No," Celia said with a small frown. "That stupid branch is stuck to my mirror." She moved her hand to the door. "Be a dear and reach out there and tug it off, will you Agnes?"

Flo and Agnes realized at the same moment what Ce was about to do and they both yelled, "No!"

But Celia was already pressing the button to open the window.

Wet, soapy fabric rolled across the space where the window had been and painted the side of Agnes's head with sweet smelling soap.

Agnes held perfectly still as the slap, slap, slap of soapy cloth danced its way across her neck and shoulders, spraying soapy liquid in a wide arc across both Flo and Agnes.

"Grab the branch, Agnes," Celia said in an irritated voice. "You're getting my car all wet."

The soapy arms rolled on down the car, and they were heading for the rinse zone. Flo shoved soap off her face and tried to refluff her bouff. "Close the window, Ce."

"Just reach out and..." Celia didn't get a chance to finish that sentence.

Quick as a whip, Agnes reached out and snagged the branch, dragging it free of the mirror. She turned on Ce, a wild glint in her eye, holding the soapy sapling up between them as if she were considering bludgeoning their clueless friend with it.

Celia's sense of self-preservation finally kicked in, and her eyes went wide. Moving very slowly, as if confronted with a wild animal, she pressed two fingers against the button on the door. The window behind Agnes rolled silently upward, hitting the top just as the rinse arms began dropping gallons of water over the car.

Celia and Agnes faced off for a long moment, Agnes's chest heaving as she struggled with her anger. Soapy water dripped steadily off her graying brown bob and saturated her cotton shirt.

A drop of water clung to the end of her nose, bobbling with every heaving breath she took.

Flo thought she should probably try to diffuse the situation. But she was afraid to break the spell between the two combatants, fearing Agnes would go all Viking Berserker on Celia.

She wasn't sure how much damage her enraged friend could do with a soggy sapling. But Flo was unwilling to find out.

Finally, Agnes opened her mouth and spoke slowly and clearly, twitching the branch for emphasis on every word. "You. Will. Drive. Like. A. Sane. Person. Now."

Celia's eyes were wide. Unblinking. She swallowed hard and then gave a little nod of her head.

The dryers blasted water off the shiny surface of Ce's new death trap, and the car oozed to the end of the line and stopped as the small stop light turned from red to green.

Just beyond the door, the white pickup gunned it, laying rubber in an attempt to get out ahead of Celia Andretti.

But Ce put the car into gear and very sedately eased out into the lot and onto the road.

Agnes lowered the branch and turned to face forward, her broad shoulders finally easing.

Flo took a deep breath and closed her eyes, leaning her head against the seat.

Finally believing she might survive the day.

"WHAT IN THE WORLD?" Nanna Potts gasped as the three women trudged into her home.

Flo shoved self-consciously at the flat spot in her bouff. "Don't ask, hun."

Nanna scanned a look over Agnes and frowned. "Is that a new hairstyle, Agnes?"

"Yeah, I call it Trip through the Car Wash," Agnes said, glaring at Celia.

Their friend shrugged, unconcerned. "I'm so sorry for your loss," Celia told Nanna.

"Thank you, dear. It's been quite the shock. And now with Davey deciding to take his father's place in the campaign..." She expelled a long sigh, her face a mask of worry. "Everything's moving so fast."

"Whatever made him decide to run for mayor," Flo asked the other woman. "Becoming mayor for a small town like Silver City is a far cry from being a successful Financial Planner in Indianapolis."

"I know. I tried to talk him out of it. But, with his father gone, I think he feels like he should move back to keep an eye on me."

"Has he..." Flo frowned, unsure how to warn Nanna without totally freaking her out. "I mean, we don't know why his father was killed yet."

Nanna fixed a weary gaze on Flo, not seeming to comprehend her message.

Flo couldn't bring herself to elaborate and terrify the poor woman. She'd discuss it with young David instead. Maybe she could talk some sense into him. "Nanna, I was wondering if you could give us any more information about the woman we discussed before. I went to the Potts Farms offices but I couldn't get access to her. The woman behind the Information desk was very circumspect."

Nanna nodded. "Her name is Audrey Macintosh. Like the apple." Nanna curled her lip. "It sounds like a stripper name, doesn't it? Horrible woman."

Flo patted Nanna's hand. "Thank you. I'm hoping to run her to ground tomorrow. What time do the offices open?"

"Mother?"

Nanna turned with a smile as a young man came into the room, scanning a suspicious glance over Flo and her friends. "Pet, dear. Come and meet these wonderful ladies. They're here to offer condolences."

Nanna gave Flo a quick glance filled with meaning. She didn't want her son to know she was investigating his father's murder. Flo didn't blame her.

"Hello, Pet. You probably don't remember me."

The young man grinned. "Mrs. Bee. My favorite substitute teacher."

"How are you doing, Peter? It's nice to see you again." Flo beamed with genuine pleasure. She took his hand, his grip gentle and slightly moist. He wasn't very tall, probably five feet ten or eleven, like his father had been. And the resemblance to David Potts didn't stop there. Like his father, Peter Potts tended slightly to pudgy, and his round head was covered in a wild halo of thick, dark hair. But unlike his father, Peter kept the heavy beard on his jawline short and tidy.

Peter scanned a look toward Nanna. "Mom, where are your manners? Have you offered the ladies a seat or refreshment?"

Nanna became instantly flustered. "Oh, dear. You're right. Please, sit. Can I get you some tea?"

"I'd love a cook..." Agnes stopped, frowning. "Maybe just some carrot sticks?"

Poor Agnes.

"I'll help," Celia offered, wrapping an arm around the other woman and throwing Flo a look over her shoulder.

Flo nodded. Ce would keep Nanna in the kitchen as long as she could so Flo could question Pet. It was clear the young man had something he wanted to ask or tell Flo, which was why he'd so brutally dispatched his mother.

Agnes wandered around while Flo and Pet walked over to sit down on a long, lemon-yellow couch. The room was good-sized, open and light, with a wall of French doors that looked out over a patio and a beautiful landscape of grass and trees.

"This is a lovely spot," Flo told Pet as she sat down on the couch. He sat down next to her, flinging a glance in the direction Ce and Nan had gone before fixing Flo with a worried look. "We don't have much time, Mrs. Bee. I need to talk to you about dad's murder."

Flo didn't bother trying to pretend David wasn't murdered. Obviously, his son saw things clearly. "I'm so sorry, Peter. It's a horrible thing."

He nodded, frowning. "I'm worried about mom." He hesitated a beat. "And David. What if dad was killed to make way for someone else in the race? I know politics can be ruthless."

Flo didn't deny the possibility. She really couldn't, since she'd had the very same thought. "I'm looking into that, Peter. But I really wish your brother hadn't jumped into the race so quickly."

Peter nodded, his expression slightly smug.

Flo realized her mistake immediately. "I mean—I'm just asking around. Because I feel so badly for your mother."

Peter shook his head. "Don't bother, Mrs. Bee. I know that you've been involved investigating some recent crimes. And from what I hear, you've been pretty successful." He frowned. "I'm worried about you too, though, Mrs. Bee. Whoever did that to dad is a cold-blooded killer. You shouldn't be mixed up in this thing either."

"Don't worry about me, hun. I'm very careful. And I have Agnes." Flo grinned, nodding toward her large friend, who was cocking her head at an African tribal mask hanging on the wall. Agnes heard her name and turned, lifting her hand to Pet. "Hello."

"Hi." He stood up and walked over, using a thick finger to straighten the mask just slightly. "Ugly thing, isn't it? The parental units spent two months in Africa last year. They came back with all sorts of horrible collectibles."

Agnes nodded. "It's definitely unique."

Pet laughed. "That's a word for it, yes." He turned back to Flo. "Mrs. Bee, I hope you'll keep me informed on the investigation? Just so I can make sure Mom and David are safe?"

Since Flo didn't want to make that promise, she distracted him instead. "Do you have any idea who might have wanted to harm your father?" she asked Pet.

"You mean, besides Christopher Chisholm?" Pet shook his head. "I loved my dad, Mrs. Bee, but I wasn't blind to his faults. He stepped on a lot of toes as a businessman, and I expect that suspect list would be pretty long. But if you're asking me who would be mad enough, or stood to gain enough from his death to kill him, I'd have to say, Mr. Chisholm. If dad had succeeded in his coup attempt, Chisholm's Chicken would have gone bankrupt. I'd say that's a pretty good reason to kill somebody. Wouldn't you?"

CHAPTER FOURTEEN

"DID YOU LEARN ANYTHING useful?" Ce asked Flo on their, thankfully, sedate drive across town.

Flo nodded. "Young Peter isn't thrilled that his brother is running against Vlad either. Though, surprisingly, he didn't point the finger at Vlad for his father's murder."

"Obviously he hasn't met the vamp then."

"Word," Celia said in agreement. "Where exactly is this emergency vet, Flo?"

"Baker Street. Just off the highway. You can't miss it. There's a giant dog statue on the front lawn."

"The Bulldog?" Agnes asked with a grin. "I love that statue."

Flo turned to the back seat, nodding. "Me too. There's just something about bulldogs that make me giggle."

"If Peter Potts doesn't blame Vlad, who *does* he think killed his dad?" Celia asked.

"Christopher Chisholm."

Celia turned to Flo, her blue eyes wide. "Really? Oh my."

"What is it, Ce? Do you know him?"

"I do, actually. Mass and I have known Chris and Megan for years. We occasionally go out together. They're nice enough people."

"Is he too nice to kill?" Flo asked.

Celia gave that some serious thought. Finally, she nodded. "In my opinion, yes. He's kind of a milquetoast."

"Anybody's capable of killing under the right circumstances," Agnes put in from the back seat.

"That's true," Flo agreed, nodding. "Though it's a lot easier to see some as killers than others."

"Exactly," Celia agreed. "And speaking of bulldogs, if I were going to pick one of the Chisholms to be a killer, it would definitely be Megan. She's the brains and the brawn in that relationship."

Flo was surprised. Then she chastised herself. She shouldn't be surprised to find out a woman was a murderer. Women killed all the time. But murder by ax was a bit gruesome for your average woman, no matter how murderous she was. "Do you think Megan Chisholm could have lopped David Potts's head off?"

Celia grimaced. "I guess if he was subdued somehow. She's not a tiny woman, but she's no Amazon either."

Celia had misunderstood Flo's question. Flo had been asking if Megan was mentally and emotionally equipped to murder so brutally. But the physical aspects were important too. "You bring up a good point, Ce," Flo told her. "For a woman to kill a man as big as Potts like he was killed, she'd have to either knock him out or drug him."

Celia nodded, taking the turn into the emergency vet clinic.

"I'll go talk to Detective Peters tomorrow. Maybe we can talk him into telling us if Potts was drugged."

They drove past a fifteen-foot tall grinning bulldog with a sling on one beefy leg. Flo smiled.

"Or you could just talk to my friend Andy," Celia said. She pulled the car into a space at the front of the lot and put it in Park.

"Your friend?" Flo asked, confused.

"Andy's a forensic pathologist at the morgue."

Flo's eyes went wide. "Ce! Why didn't you tell me you had a friend at the morgue?"

Celia gave her a stunned look. "That's not exactly the kind of thing that comes up in regular conversation, Flo."

"Can you ask her if she'll see me tomorrow?"

"Of course."

Flo patted her friend's arm. "Thanks, hun. That's great news." She reached for the door handle and gave Ce a last look before climbing out. "You two go on back. I'll call a taxi or an Uber or something to get back."

"We can wait," Celia said with a smile. "I don't mind."

"Don't be silly. I'm going to sit with my little man for a bit. I don't want you sitting out here waiting. I'm sure you have better things to do."

"If you're sure..."

Flo nodded. "Perfectly sure. Thanks so much for driving me around today, hun. I really appreciate it." Flo peered into the back seat. "Will you take my shoes inside, Agnes?" Flo had found the perfect pair of bowling shoes at the sports store. Agnes had found some too, though hers were less perfect.

"Sure."

"Thanks. I'll see you ladies later."

FIFTEEN MINUTES LATER, Flo was seated in a small room with an exam table and a cushioned bench. The door opened and a young woman came in, carrying a groggy looking Rodney in her arms. She smiled at Flo. "He's been agitated. We gave him a little sedative. He's probably going to be a little sleepy."

Flo took note of the bandage on the girl's finger. "Please tell me he didn't do that?"

She laughed it off. "It's just a little nip. No biggie. I've had much worse." She handed Rodney to Flo. "I'll be back in a half hour. It will be time for his dinner then."

Rodney whined softly as Flo buried her face in his soft red fur. "Hello, little man. Are you feeling any better?"

The dachshund's tongue came out and swiped across her nose in response.

She laughed softly. "I'll take that as a yes."

The door opened again and a woman in a white coat came inside. She held a clipboard, and the name on her coat marked her as the veterinarian. She offered Flo her hand. "Hello, Mrs. Bee. I'm Doctor Alyson. Your little dog was pretty sick."

"Is he going to be okay?"

"He is. In fact, I think you can bring him home in the morning."

"Oh, that's good news," Flo said, hugging Rodney close.

He lifted weary brown eyes to the vet and gave a soft growl.

Doctor Alyson laughed, unconcerned. "He's not a fan of being here."

"No, he likes his ducks in a row."

"Well, dachshunds are very fond of their people and nobody else, generally." Her smile was genuine. She observed the cranky doxie with a warm gaze. "He'll be happy to get back to his bed and toys. I'm sending him home with antibiotics. I want him resting for the first few days at least. His old body has been taxed by this, and it will take him a bit longer to recover fully. But I don't see why he shouldn't be a hundred percent by next week at this time."

"That's wonderful news."

The vet scribbled something on her clipboard and then glanced at Flo. "Do you have any questions for me?"

Flo cocked her head. "Yes. But it's probably not what you expect. Have we met before? You look very familiar."

The young woman grinned. "I wasn't sure if you'd remember me, Mrs. Bee."

The mischievous smile triggered a memory in Flo. She let her eyes go wide. "Talya Alyson. Of course, the first name for a last name should have clicked with me right away." She laughed. "I would have never recognized you. You've changed so much."

"I was thirty pounds overweight, with acne and braces," Doctor Alyson said, shaking her head. "I'm not surprised you didn't recognize me."

"You were beautiful," Flo told her with a straight face. "All my little ducklings were beautiful."

The veterinarian chuckled good-naturedly. "Why, Mrs. Bee, I never realized what a good liar you are."

Flo barked out a laugh. "Behave." Rodney let out a snore and Flo shifted him so she'd be more comfortable, leaning back on the bench. "As I recall, you were best friends with Peter Potts."

She nodded. "We both took a beating for the name thing. It brought us closer."

When Flo looked a question at her, Doctor Alyson said, "PeePee Potts? Are you telling me you never heard him called that?"

"Oh, my. That's not good."

"No," the young vet agreed, shaking her head. "I'm afraid poor Peter had some anger issues back then. I can't say I blame him."

"Have you kept in touch?" Flo asked, wondering if the young woman had heard about David Pott's murder.

"Not so much," she responded. She pressed the clipboard to her chest and wrapped her arms around it. "I ran into him a few weeks ago though. I was happy to hear he was in med school. Peter is very smart. He'll make a great doctor."

"Have you heard about his father?"

Talya frowned a question. A moment later, horror replaced the confusion. "Oh. I'll admit I hadn't made the connection. There are actually several Potts's in Silver City. That was his dad?"

"I'm afraid so."

"How horrible for him and for his mother. She's such a wonderful person." Talya's expressive face took on a nostalgic look. "She used to bake us cookies for after school snacks. She'd wait until we walked in the door to put them in the oven so they'd be hot and gooey when we dove into them." Talya shook her head. "She must be devastated."

"She's handling it as well as can be expected, but I'm afraid the boys aren't making things any easier. At least David isn't."

"Why? What's he done?"

Flo realized she'd spoken out of turn and shook her head. "I probably shouldn't have said anything. It's not my place. The information hasn't been made public yet. I expect it will be announced soon enough."

To her credit, the young vet didn't press. "Those activists probably aren't helping things."

"The animal rights activists?" Flo asked. She nodded. "Mrs. Potts told me about them. I haven't seen them yet though."

"I think they're focusing on Chisholm's right now. They alternate between the two farms." Talya shook her head. "Between you and me, those people are cray. I went to college with one of them. She hates people but would throw herself in front of a bullet for a sewer rat."

"I understand their concern," Flo said, frowning. "There's so much cruelty in the world. If I could stop even a fraction of it, I might decide to hit the streets too."

Talya nodded. "So would I. But when you start threatening people..." She sighed. "I'll be happier when they get tired of harassing Silver City and move on."

Flo agreed. She made a mental note to talk to Detective Peters about the activists.

Talya extended her hand, smiling. "It was nice seeing you again, Mrs. Bee. If you have any concerns about your little dog feel free to give me a call." She held a business card between two fingers. "My cell phone number is on the back. Call any time of the night or day, okay?"

"Thank you, hun. I'm sure Rodney will be just fine."

Doctor Alyson nodded and left.

Flo snuggled with Rodney until the tech came back to fetch him for his dinner. Her mind spun with everything going on in the world of chickens and chicken processors. It seemed much too big a coincidence that David Potts was killed at the same time the activists were in the area. Their disappearing immediately following his death seemed too big a coincidence too.

However, if they were the culprits, the Chisholm's should be a target too. Flo needed to try to talk to those activists. But first, she had to try again to speak to the one person who seemed to be at the center of everything.

David Potts's elusive scientist.

CHAPTER FIFTEEN

WHEN FLO LEFT THE CLINIC, a familiar 1975 Plymouth Valiant was sitting at the curb, its powerful engine purring happily.

Flo grinned when she saw the big woman sitting behind the wheel of the car. She waved and hurried over, pulling the door on the passenger side open to the sound of a throaty creak. "Cook! What are you doing here? I didn't even know you had a pet."

Cook shook her head, waving a beefy hand toward the passenger side seat. "Get on in, cher. I came ta get ya."

Flo climbed into the big car, sliding across the pristine white leather seat and reaching to drag the door closed with another creak. "I wasn't expecting anyone. I was just going to take a taxi."

"Don't be silly, cher," Cook said in her husky Cajun drawl. "I heard you was here and offered ta pick ya up. It ain't no big deal."

"I'm delighted." She rubbed a hand over the smooth leather. "I just love this car."

Cook's teeth were bright in her dark face. "Me too. Dey just don' make 'em like dis no more."

"That's certainly true."

"So how is your little man?"

"He'll be fine, hun. But he gave me quite a scare." Flo frowned, glancing at her watch. "Aren't you supposed to be in the kitchen right now?"

"Little miss Natasha is fillin' in for me today. I had an appointment wid da doctor."

Natasha Sabitov had come to Silver Hills when her brother Yegor ended up on the wrong side of a ruthless killer. Like her brother, she'd started as a dishwasher and helper in the kitchen, but, though Russian-born Natasha had started out speaking only broken English, she was getting more agile with the language every day. The young woman was smart and worked hard. She was quickly becoming indispensable to Cook. "You're not sick, I hope?" Flo asked.

Cook blew a raspberry, rolling the wide-bodied car through the turn onto Main Street in downtown Silver City. "Dis Cajun strong as an ox. Stronger. It just be time for dat pesky checkup."

"Ah. Good. You need to take good care of yourself, hun. We'd all be lost without you."

She laughed at that. "You mean Agnes be lost widout my pies."

"She certainly would. But she'd miss your sweet disposition more."

They shared a grin.

"And speaking of Agnes. I wanted to ask you something."

"Ask away, cher." Cook pulled the big car into the parking lot at Silver Hills and drove to the furthest corner, angling it into three spots so nobody could get close.

"Agnes has decided she wants to get healthy."

"Dat's good, right?"

"Very good. But she's trying to give up everything she loves, and it's making her cranky."

Cook slapped the steering wheel, laughing heartily. "I'll just bet."

"Well, I was wondering if you had any experience with sugar-free baking."

Cook fixed her wide brown gaze on Flo and stared, expression neutral, for so long Flo thought she might have inadvertently said something to offend the other woman.

"If you don't, it's no big deal. I just thought I'd ask."

"Cher, how long you know me?"

In that moment, Flo thought maybe not long enough. "I..."

"O'course I can bake widout da sugar. A woman like me takes dat as a challenge. You just give me a day or two ta figure out how ta transform dat girl's favorite pies. I'll make her some treats she won't even know is healthy."

Flo reached over and squeezed Cook's arm. "You're the best."

"Don't I know it, cher."

THE BAR ADJACENT TO the dining room was full when Flo and Cook came through the front door. The space was separated from the main room by a low, half wall that was lined with high-top round tables on the bar side. The tall stools nestled around the tables were full of people from both sides of the residence. The glossy wood bar ran the length of the wall, and every stool along its length was also filled. The group was strangely quiet, every face pointed toward the big screen TV on the wall behind the bar. Even the bartender, Dutch, appeared hypnotized by the scene playing out on the television, as he dried a tall glass with his customary white bar rag.

Flo wondered what was happening that had everyone so engrossed.

"I'll see ya later, cher." Cook veered off toward the swinging door into the residence kitchen.

Flo gave Cook a distracted thank you and headed for the bar, her gaze locked onto the handsome, somehow familiar face of the young man on the screen. He stood behind a flag-draped podium in an unrecognizable location, his thick, dark hair cut business-style-short and combed tidily to one side. His expression was intense, his gaze locked onto the camera, and his speech was filled with emotion.

The camera embraced only him, but a continual whir of flashing lights told Flo the press was also in the room.

With a jolt, Flo realized how she knew him. It was young David Potts.

She came up beside Agnes and received a quick nod of greeting before Agnes returned her attention to the screen.

"I feel it is my duty to see this through in honor of my father," David Potts Junior was saying. "His dream was to have a chance to improve the lives of Silver City's residents. He had so many ideas. Such big plans for improvements. He would have been such a wonderful mayor."

David Potts hesitated, blinking rapidly as emotion overcame him. Flo's heart broke a little for the young man. She couldn't help wondering if he was making a big mistake, throwing himself into the ruthless world of politics so soon after his father's murder.

"My father was a big thinker. He loved to challenge himself, and he always strived to go beyond what others thought was possible. He was a proud man, almost to a fault, and sometimes he could come off as brusque. He had a tendency to rub people the wrong way. But that was because he was passionate over the things he cared about." Potts stopped talking for a beat and leaned over the podium, his dark eyes filled with intensity. "I care about those same things. And I intend to see my father's dreams realized here in Silver City. I will work vigorously to improve the condition of our roads. I'll be a relentless supporter of our schools and teachers. I'll be a tireless advocate for our first responders, ensuring they have the resources they need to keep us all safe. And on a personal level, for you and for me, I vow to make sure that the man who killed my father pays for his horrific crime."

A low murmur filled the room around him. There was scattered applause that didn't find purchase in the room. Agnes and Flo shared a look.

"I know what some of you are thinking. That I should leave that work to our wonderful police department. I fully intend to do that. But I won't keep my mouth shut about my suspicions. I've already told the police who I believe killed my father. I will monitor their work closely to ensure they stay on the trail until the killer is behind bars." He hesitated for a beat and then jabbed a finger toward the camera. "And, most importantly, I won't let him win. I intend to beat my opponent in November so that the mayor of this great city will be named David Potts. As it always should have been."

The room where young Potts stood erupted into cheering. The camera panned over a standing crowd of what looked like hundreds of flushed and red-eyed people. Flo figured he was probably addressing his father's donors and campaign staff.

Then it hit her. David Junior's words. He'd said he would beat the killer in November. She turned to Agnes and saw the moment her friend grasped the meaning of his words too.

Young David Potts had just publically accused Vladwicke Newsome of brutally murdering his father.

"I STILL CAN'T BELIEVE he accused the vamp of murder," Celia said, shaking her head. She ran perfect red nails through the short strands of her silky blonde hair and picked up her wine glass. "Though I don't disagree the man's capable of murder. It's still shocking."

"Do you really think so?" Flo asked. When Ce looked up at her, she clarified. "Do you really believe Vlad's capable of murder?"

Ce shrugged. She stared at the amber liquid in her glass, swirling it absently. "I guess, even with all the joking we do about him, I really don't believe it. Deep down."

Agnes climbed a stool across from Flo, a wide grin on her face and a frosty glass of beer in her hand. "I'm in the pool."

"Pool?" Flo asked.

Ce frowned. "Did I miss an activity notice? I thought we had bowling tonight."

Agnes rolled her eyes. "You two are oblivious. The pool for when Vlad gets arrested for Potts's murder."

"That's terrible!" Flo said, slapping her friend's hand.

Agnes chuckled.

Celia didn't say anything. When Flo looked at her, she seemed to be contemplating something.

"There's still a few dates left," Agnes told their friend.

Celia settled her glass onto the table and picked up her tiny clutch purse. "I'll just..." She climbed down from the tall stool. Looking at Flo, she said, "I'm just going to the ladies." Ce started toward the restrooms, veering at the last minute toward the small group clustered around a sign-up sheet on the bar.

"You're awful," Flo said, but her lips twitched despite her attempt to be outraged. "You know Vlad didn't kill that man, right?"

Agnes shrugged. "I see no reason why the vamp shouldn't provide some much-needed entertainment for the hoards. And maybe make me a little money while he's at it."

Flo sighed. Then she remembered her visitor from that morning. "I met your young man this morning."

Agnes's round cheeks pinkened prettily. Her gaze slid away. "I don't have a young man."

"Well, he'd like to have you." Then realizing how that had sounded, Flo hurried to append it. "I mean, I think he really likes you, hun."

Agnes grinned despite herself. "I really like him too."

"Good. That's good." Flo sipped from her glass of red wine. "Is he coming tonight?"

"To bowling? I have no idea. I hope not."

"Why not? It would be a perfect first date. You'd be surrounded by other people and doing something fun."

Agnes fixed Flo with a quelling look. "It wouldn't be a date. It would be an opportunity for him to see me as a first class clown. You know I can't bowl."

Unfortunately, it was true. As big and strong as Agnes was, she didn't seem able to coordinate all her limbs long enough to move the ball down the alley and into the pins. "It's not about winning. It's about spending time with friends."

Agnes blew air through her lips. "Tell that to Roger."

Flo wisely didn't respond. Roger hadn't been thrilled to learn their group had gained Agnes when the teams were assigned. What Flo didn't tell him was that she herself had asked TC to add Agnes to their team. If she hadn't, Agnes was in terrible danger of being that one kid who wasn't picked for any of the teams. As popular as Agnes was with the other residents, everybody had seen her bowl at the last outing and nobody wanted that train wreck on their team. What kind of friend would she be if she abandoned Agnes in her time of need?

"Well, I'm glad you're on our team. We're going to have lots of fun. Roger and Celia are ace bowlers. I'm not great, but I'll get us a few points. There won't be any pressure at all on you to do anything but have fun."

Agnes didn't look convinced. She sipped her beer and then, catching Flo's eye, quickly explained. "This is Lite beer, low on carbs. It's almost like drinking water."

Flo lifted her brows. "You don't say?"

"I do say, Flo." In a naked attempt to change the subject, Agnes asked, "So, are we going to talk to David Potts tomorrow?"

"We need to talk to him at some point. But to be honest, I'd rather talk to that scientist first. She seems to be at the center of everything."

Agnes nodded. "Sounds good. What time do you want to go?"

"I have to see about my car." Flo's eyes went wide. She'd totally forgotten about getting her car fixed. "Oh no. I didn't call about getting new tires."

"No worries, doll."

Agnes and Flo turned as Roger strolled up and lowered himself onto a tall stool. "Richard and I took care of it. I hope you don't mind."

"Oh Roger, you're such a dear. But you really shouldn't have."

"I should have and did. What else are friends for?"

Agnes waggled her brows. "Flo and Roger sitting in a tree..."

"Hush, fool," Flo said as she blushed.

Roger laughed. "I don't suppose you could go get me one of those beers, Agnes?"

"Sure. Should I just have Dutch put it on your tab?"

"That would be perfect. Thanks, young lady."

Flo eyed him as Agnes returned to the bar. She was drawn like a moth to the flame back to the energetic "pool" group, which Flo noticed still included one Celia Angonetti. "If you hurry, you still might be able to get a date in the pool for when Vlad will be arrested," she told Roger.

He shook his head. "Children."

She grinned and he smiled back, clasping her hand in his big, warm grip. "I missed you today. What did you girls get up to?"

Flo filled him in on the visit to the Potts home and her conversation with Peter Potts.

Roger sat in thoughtful silence until she was finished. "There's something on the edge of my memory about young Peter."

"Legal trouble?" Flo asked.

"I believe so. Oh, I remember. He was in a bar fight in college. It didn't amount to anything legally. Both boys came away with black eyes and bruises. David Potts paid for all the damage, so nobody was interested in filing charges. I believe Peter takes after his father in one way at least. He has a bit of a temper."

"Speaking of angry Potts kids, did you happen to see David Potts Junior's presser a while ago?"

"I did," Roger verified. "A bit unexpected for him to call out Newsome that way."

"It was."

"You know, there's another way to interpret what he said."

"There is?"

"Yes. He might have just been saying that, if the killer was trying to keep David Potts from becoming mayor, he wasn't going to get his wish because young David fully intended to serve as his replacement, instituting his father's agenda in David Senior's stead."

Flo thought about that. "You're right. That could have been what he was saying. I guess we all heard what we expected to hear."

"Or you were right, and he said what everybody thought they heard. I guess you won't know until you talk to the lad."

"Yes. And I intend to do that soon." But it had occurred to Flo that there was someone else she needed to talk to before she had a conversation with Ms. Macintosh or young Potts.

And that someone was currently exiting the manager's office with his wife Vampira, a.k.a. Morticia, a.k.a Morty Newsome.

CHAPTER SIXTEEN

"VLAD, I'D LIKE TO TALK to you," Flo called out as she hurried toward the couple.

The nasty night manager frowned in her direction and glanced toward the door as if considering ducking back inside to avoid talking to Flo.

But Morty squared her shoulders and lifted her chin, looking down her long, straight nose at Flo. "We have nothing to say to you."

Flo stopped in front of them, giving Morty a pointed look. "You can either set the record straight with me, or allow the overactive rumor mill in the building to run with the innuendo spawned from David Junior's press conference."

Morty's black gaze narrowed on Flo, her thin lips tightening with pique. Finally, she sighed, glancing toward her husband. "You might as well tell her so she'll leave us alone."

Not a very gracious concession, but Flo would take any cross in a vamp storm. "I'll help you clear your name if you're innocent."

Vlad's lips curled with contempt. His sneer rose all the way to his dark gaze, which was fixed on her as if she were a particularly repulsive bug smashed on the bottom of his shoe. "I don't need to prove I'm innocent. I've done nothing wrong."

"Nothing?" Flo asked, arching an eyebrow.

Morty shifted slightly, just enough to draw Flo's gaze in her direction. "Nothing," she repeated, though her denial lacked some of the conviction Vlad's had. "Morty, what do you know?"

She flashed Vlad a look that had a tinge of apology in it. "How was I supposed to know the man would be murdered?"

Vlad's sneer turned in her direction, softening only slightly. "What did you do?" he asked his wife.

Morty twitched under his perusal. It was strangely uncomfortable for Flo to see the usually overly confident, cool under pressure, Vampira so discombobulated. "It was entirely innocent."

"Tell me, Morty," Flo said in a subdued tone. "If it was innocent as you say, I'll help with damage control."

"And why would you do that?" Vlad snarled. "Why would you help us? You hate us as much as we hate you."

Morty frowned just enough to tell Flo the other woman didn't have a two-way ticket on Vlad's Hate Train.

"I don't hate you. Well, I don't hate Morty. You, I just don't like. A lot."

"What's the difference?"

"It's admittedly very small," Flo acknowledged. "But it's there. Even if I did hate you, I wouldn't want to see you blamed for something you didn't do."

"He didn't do it, Flo."

The trace of fear in Morty's voice had Flo scanning a look her way.

The other woman leaned closer, lowering her voice. "I had a slight altercation with David Potts at the mall a few days ago."

Concern brought a chill to Flo's spine. "A *public* altercation?"

Morty hesitated a beat and then nodded.

"What was the fight about?"

"Just the usual, inter-campaign stuff. Nothing dire. I promise."

"What exactly did you say to the victim?"

She gave Flo the stink eye over her choice of words, but answered the question. "I might have implied that Vlad was going to take him down."

Flo closed her eyes. "Oh, Morty."

"Well, how was I to know someone would actually do the man in two days later?" Morty retreated back into her usual arrogance beneath Flo's unspoken judgment.

Flo gave the information a moment to sink in. Then she turned to Vlad. "Okay, we're still all right as long as they have no physical evidence against you."

Vlad's gaze slid away and worry twisted through her belly. "What?"

Vlad shook his head. "Stay out of our business, old woman. I won't tell you again." He slammed the door to the manager's office behind him, leaving a shocked Flo standing with an equally shocked Morty.

Flo recovered first. "What's going on?" she asked the other woman.

Morty twisted her fingers in front of her, her gaze sliding toward the bar. Many of the patrons were staring across the lobby at them.

Vlad's outburst had been loud enough to cut into their revelry.

"Morty? I really am trying to help."

Finally, Morty said, "Ask Preston. It was his bright idea." Then she turned around and followed her husband into the office.

Flo heard the click of the lock turning behind her.

As if on cue, the front door opened and Detective Brent Peters strode into the lobby.

Spying him, Agnes smacked the big guy next to her on the arm, and they descended on the pool calendar together.

Peters did a slow scan of the common area and then slid his gaze over the bar crowd before turning to Flo with a frown.

Flo wondered if the Detective's frown was because of her, or if it had more to do with not seeing a certain young and pretty activities director in the vicinity. She waved and, somewhat reluctantly it seemed, he started toward her.

"How are you tonight, Detective?"

He stopped a couple of feet away and gave her a hard stare. "I'd be better if I didn't think you were messing around in my murder case, Mrs. Bee."

"I've been hired to find out who killed him, Detective. But I'm only gathering information. I promise."

He didn't look convinced. "I shouldn't need to tell you that the person we're looking for is very dangerous. What he did to David Potts..." Peters paled slightly.

Flo realized the murder had been graphic enough to stun even the police. That made her feel better about horking up her lunch at the scene. "I'll pass anything I learn onto you."

"Mm, hm. I'm going to take you up on that." He hooked his thumbs in the pockets of his jeans. "What did you learn just now from your very scary night managers?"

"I don't think he did it, Detective."

Peters frowned. "Of course you don't."

"Hey, I'm not overly fond of Vladwicke Newsome. You of all people should know that."

Peters inclined his head. "I do. But the devil you know is sometimes too familiar to recognize for what he is."

"You believe young David Potts's accusation?" she asked him.

"I wasn't aware he made an accusation against anyone?"

"Right. I guess your showing up here a mere hour after his press conference is just a coincidence?"

Shrugging, Peters gave Flo cop face. "Must be."

"And you're asking *me* for honesty." She shook her head in disgust.

"I am. In fact, I'm insisting on it. So, tell me what the Newsome's just told you."

She considered holding out but decided the best way to gain the Detective's trust and acceptance as an investigator was to appear cooperative.

That was exactly what she'd do. *Appear* cooperative. "Morty admitted she'd had an argument with Potts a couple of days ago. She insists it was nothing but a little healthy rivalry."

Something changed in the young detective's face, and Flo realized his question had been a test. "You already knew about the fight?"

"Thanks for the information, Mrs. Bee."

She bit back irritation and stepped closer, lowering her voice. "I had a thought."

He lifted a brow, waiting.

"Those activists. Do you think they might have killed Potts? From what I've heard, they're a bit radical."

His expression tightened with irritation. He thought she was questioning his work. "I'm looking at that."

"I was just thinking, if they killed Potts, the Chisholms might be next."

Peters's eyes went wide. His mouth fell open in a shocked "Oh". He smacked his hand against his forehead. "Why? Why didn't I think of that?"

Flo rolled her eyes. "Okay, I get it."

He dropped the act, glowering down at her. "No, I don't think you *do* get it. I know what I'm doing, Flo. I've been doing this policing thing for a while now."

She raised her hands in surrender. "Okay."

He relaxed subtly.

"But would you at least tell me about these activists? Nanna's worried about them, and I'd like to reassure her."

"Reassure her? No. Those people are a few fries short of a happy meal. But I checked each and every one of them out. None of them has a record of violence."

"Do they have other records?"

His jaw tightened, but he pushed through the irritation. "Petty larceny. Car theft, time served. One woman punched her boyfriend out at a bar because he wouldn't let her have a puppy." Peters lifted a golden eyebrow. "These aren't people you'd want to hang out with, Mrs. Bee. Mrs. Potts, the

Chisholms, and you should all stay away from them. But it would be a stretch to assume one of them is a murderer."

She couldn't resist one last question. "The Chisholms and David Potts's family are safe?"

"I have no idea," he said irritably. "Lightning could flash down and kill them tomorrow."

Frustration kept Flo silent.

Peters knocked on the office door. "Stay well away from this killer, Mrs. Bee. I mean it."

"You ready to go?" Agnes asked, striding up to them with a glance at Peters. "Hey, Detective."

"Miss Willard."

"Are you here to arrest Vlad?"

Flo rolled her eyes.

"Not today."

Agnes turned to the bar. "Not today!" she shouted out. There was general grumbling, and the group fell upon the pool again. The man Agnes had smacked on the arm tore up a piece of paper in disgust. She winked at Flo. "Too bad. Hey, if you could wait a few days to arrest him. Like maybe Saturday, I'd really appreciate it."

Peters's lips twitched. "How much is the pool?"

"A hundred dollars. But the late crowd hasn't come down yet."

He nodded. "Good luck."

"Thanks." She turned to Flo. "Ce's driving us." She grimaced. "We might need to yell at her again to remind her not to drive like Celia Andretti."

"Where are you off to?" Peters asked suspiciously.

"Not to find a murderer, if that's what you're thinking," Flo grumbled.

"It's bowling night," Agnes told him with a sour look on her face.

"Is Tricia going too?"

Flo was surprised he asked. He usually tried to play it cool. It was probably a sign of his misery that the words had escaped. Sure enough, as soon as he asked the question, the detective looked like he wanted to take them back.

"Yep. She'll be there," Flo said coolly. But the sad look on his face made her instantly regret being cavalier. "Why don't you stop by? I'm sure TC would love to see you."

For just a beat he seemed to want to agree, but then he shook his head, frowning. "I have work to do. I'll see you later, ladies."

"Come on, Flo. Celia will leave without us."

Flo allowed herself to be dragged toward the door. She was so distracted by the whole Detective Peters and TC thing she almost forgot she didn't need a ride to bowling. "No, remember, Roger got my car fixed today. I can drive us again."

"You're right. Thank heavens!" Agnes said. She shoved the front door open and allowed Flo to exit ahead of her. "I knew I liked that guy."

Flo liked him too. But that thought almost got lost in the sound of Detective Peters calling through the locked door to Vlad.

"WHY DOES THIS PLACE always smell like feet?" Agnes groused as they walked into the *Bounce and Bowl*.

"I think it smells like sweat," Celia said, wrinkling her nose. She carried her hot pink bowling ball in a hot pink bag and wore hot pink bowling shoes to match.

Flo wore the bowling shoes she'd gotten earlier in the day, but she planned on using a house ball. If she ended up bowling very often, she might consider getting herself a ball.

Agnes held the enormous pair of bowling shoes she'd found at the sporting goods store, and was frowning.

Flo patted her friend's arm. "Don't look so unhappy. This is supposed to be fun."

"Remember that when I stink up the place and you all have perfect scores."

Flo shook her head. Glancing around the noisy bowling alley, she was unable to spot Roger. Or, for that matter, anyone else from Silver Hills.

"Florence Bee," his familiar voice called out.

Flo looked up and smiled as Roger headed toward her from the snack area. "There you are. I was starting to think we'd come to the wrong place."

He shook his head. "The kids are on our lanes. We need to wait for them to clear out."

Flo cast her gaze over the last two lanes in the building, where a buzzing hoard of small children clustered in noisy, jittering groups that the adults they were with were having trouble controlling.

Flo smiled. She remembered outings as a teacher. They were always exhausting affairs.

"Would you like something to drink?" Roger asked.

"No thanks." She thought about it and realized she would like some water. "Maybe just a glass of water."

Roger nodded and dropped a warm hand onto her back. He glanced toward Agnes, a question in his gaze.

"I'm fine," she told him. "I'm going to go pick out my ball."

Celia was already in the snack area, holding court with the mix of Silver Hills bowlers. Flo recognized a few of the women from their yoga classes and some of the men from the dining room. She greeted several people and then followed Roger to the counter.

"Two glasses of water, please," he told the woman behind the counter.

A high-pitched scream went up, causing Roger to jump and expel air. The woman behind the bar smiled. "Sorry about that. The toddlers will leave with the other kids." She nodded toward the giant bounce house that took up the corner just to the side of the snack area.

Flo took note of the cluster of young mothers who were chatting together around the house, keeping one eye on the toddlers and the other on the older siblings doing bumper bowling.

"What a fun thing for young families," Flo told the woman as she handed them two glasses of water.

"It's very popular. Before we added the bounce portion of our entertainment, the mothers and toddlers tended to hang out in here. Trust me when I tell you it's better to have them out there."

Flo and Roger chuckled.

The television on the back wall suddenly showed a snippet of the presser Flo had watched earlier. She nudged Roger. "There's David Potts again."

The woman behind the bar turned around and glanced up at it. "Do you know him?"

"I do, actually. I was his substitute teacher in high school."

"Really? Do you think he'd make a good mayor?"

Flo hesitated just long enough for the woman to take the wrong meaning. "I have my doubts too. I'm afraid he's too young."

"Youth can be a good thing," Roger offered. "He might look at things with a fresh eye."

"That's true," she said, frowning slightly. "I was going to vote for his daddy. I guess I might vote for him too. I mean, he can't be worse than that other guy, right?"

The woman's voice was so full of venom when she spoke of Vlad, Flo had to bite her tongue against the need to defend him. "You don't like Mr. Newsome?"

"I wasn't wild about him to start with, but now that I know he's a murderer."

Flo and Roger shared a glance.

"There's no proof he killed David Potts."

"No, but the son obviously thinks he did. It makes you wonder, right?"

Roger, bless his heart, shook his head. "I'm waiting for the results of the investigation. As a lawyer, I saw too many people convicted in the court of public opinion. Some of them were innocent. There's nothing more terrifying than being wrongly convicted on rumor and hearsay and being unable to do anything about it."

"Well..." The woman was clearly unhappy with Roger's opinion, but Flo was proud of him for giving it. As the woman behind the counter walked away to serve someone else, Flo turned to him. "That was a very impassioned defense of Vlad. Do you know something I don't?"

He chuckled. "Trust me, doll. It gave me heartburn to say it. But everybody, even Vlad, deserves his day in court."

TC bounced into the snack area, her green eyes sparkling. "We're up, everybody!"

Flo turned on her stool to discover that the kids and their guardians had moved out. Two men in gray cotton uniforms were in the process of moving the bumpers out of the way.

She grabbed her water glass and followed the group down to the lanes.

"Good, you're all here," TC said, marking their names off on her clipboard. "Where's Agnes? She didn't fitz out on me, did she?"

"She's picking out a ball," Roger told TC.

They all turned to find Agnes walking toward them, holding a plain, black ball in front of her as she walked.

She caught TC's eye and waved, her new shoes smacking down on the carpet like clown shoes.

"Oh dear," Roger said. "What's she got on her feet?"

"They're men's shoes. They didn't have women's shoes in her size. I'm afraid they're way too big on her. But she insisted they'd be good enough."

TC eyed her with a pained expression. "Why is my gut telling me this won't end well?"

Even as she asked the million dollar question, a pair of boys who looked to be about nine years old bumped into Agnes hard, the rubber ball from the toy machine they'd been fighting over dropping to the ground as Agnes stumbled sideways.

She threw out a hand to catch herself on the shoe rental counter and managed to keep from falling. But the bowling ball she'd been clutching escaped from her compromised grip and slammed to the ground, landing right on Agnes's foot.

"Oh!"

"Ouch!"

"No!"

TC, Flo, and Roger exclaimed in horror.

The two boys took one look at the unfortunate landing zone and took off running, slowing only long enough to scoop up the toy they'd been fighting over.

Agnes stared down at her foot, suspiciously unreactive.

"Is she in shock?" TC asked.

"That has to hurt," Flo said.

"I'd say she'll have broken toes," Roger agreed, nodding. "We'll need to run her to the emergency room."

Sighing wearily, TC started scribbling on her sheet. "I'll need to re-swizzle the teams."

But to Flo's shock, Agnes simply shrugged and reached down for the ball, plucking it off her foot and heading in their direction.

She wasn't even limping.

"Are you okay, hun?" Flo asked, hurrying up to her.

"I'm fine. The ball landed on my shoe. It didn't even touch my toes."

Everybody looked down at the flattened toe of Agnes's new bowling shoe. There looked to be about three inches of empty space in front of Agnes's toes.

TC was too relieved to even comment. "Okay, everybody. Let's get started!"

CHAPTER SEVENTEEN

FLO HELD THE BALL UP and eyed the pins. She'd had a pretty good night so far, but her last two turns at the foul line had resulted in splits. She was looking at a seven and ten at the moment, with no hope of knocking off a clean sweep.

She was deeply aware of Celia and Roger watching her. They'd both bowled near perfect games, and they needed Flo to hold up her end of the match because Agnes had been a total disaster.

Though they were much too kind to make Agnes feel badly about it.

Unfortunately, they hadn't gone out of their way to give Flo a pass on her splits. Flo knew she was being a little unfair. Her friends hadn't said or done anything to make her feel inadequate.

She'd done that entirely on her own.

Constant celebration and cheering from the Eagles in the next alley wasn't helping the mood or the stress level. As good as Roger and Celia were, they couldn't carry both Flo and Agnes and beat the more experienced Silver Hills team.

For Agnes's part, she was excited by Flo's game, seeing the remaining two pins as an accomplishment, rather than a failure.

Flo wished for just a moment she could share Agnes's enthusiasm.

With a soft sigh of resignation, Flo stepped into her delivery, concentrating hard as she moved toward the foul line. Her arm-swing was good, resulting in solid follow-through that sent the ball on a promising line right for the seven. Unfortunately, it hooked before hitting the pin deck and only gave the seven pin a gentle tap. Flo held her breath as the seven wobbled a few times and then settled, still upright, as Flo's ball rolled harmlessly into the pit.

Flo hung her head in frustration. It just wasn't her day.

A big hand fell onto her shoulder. "That was a thing of beauty, Flo."

Flo looked up in shock and met Agnes's wide gaze. "The way you glided up there and put the ball right down the center. It didn't wobble or fall in those things on the side or hit the next guy over in the leg or anything."

Despite herself, Flo chuckled. It *had* been a beautiful thing until it all went awry. "Thanks, Agnes. In your defense, though, that guy was standing too close to our runway." As excuses for chaos went, it was weak.

Agnes's ball should have been on a line toward the pins rather than rolling sideways along the platform. Fortunately, the guy hadn't been part of the Silver Hills group and had limped off shortly after Agnes's unintended assault, an ugly house ball clutched in one hand.

All too often Agnes's victims reached for a cell phone to call their lawyers, and poor Roger ended up having to throw legalese at them until they gave in and settled for an apology and a fifty dollar gift card for their pain and suffering.

He wouldn't admit it, but Flo suspected Roger stocked his pockets with those cards whenever they did anything the least bit dicey with Agnes.

Of course, with Agnes, a walk down the sidewalk could turn dicey.

Roger came over and dropped an arm around Flo's shoulders, giving her a squeeze. "Tough break, doll. There must be a divot in the lane."

She chuckled. "Nice try."

"I'm up?" Agnes asked with forced enthusiasm.

Roger grimaced before turning to Agnes. "You are, young lady. I have a feeling your luck is about to change."

He had no idea.

Flo and Roger abandoned their friend on the runway, hurrying out of range before she started toward the foul line.

Snickering erupted from the alley next to theirs. Flo looked up to find TC shushing her teammates. She shrugged an apology and then tagged a young man from the singles side, urging him to move up to the platform to take his turn. Flo thought his name was Devon. They'd met in the bar at Silver Hills once or twice, and she'd found him to be an arrogant, know-it-all as only a thirty-five-year-old man can be.

Flo watched Devon settle himself into his address, knowing the result would probably be another strike. She thought from what she'd witnessed and the cheering after each time he stepped up to the foul line, that he was probably on track to go all the way.

She forced her gaze back to Agnes, fighting the urge to hide her eyes. Her friend settled into an acceptable stance, her eyes shifting nervously toward the man in the alley next to her.

Devon glanced her way too, grinning smugly before giving her a nod.

Agnes took a deep breath, squared her shoulders, and, rather than wait for him to bowl before she moved, she engaged at the same time he did.

His delivery was a thing of beauty. He finished in a flashy slide that sent his custom-made ball off in good order, forging a straight line toward the waiting pins.

Agnes's first step was perfect. Her second wasn't bad, but as she took that final step at the foul line, the toe of one of her oversized shoes got caught on the side of the other shoe, and Agnes started to go down.

With a startled cry, she threw her arms up in a desperate attempt to keep from falling flat on her face. In that first terrifying second, she managed to rebalance herself enough to avoid a full frontal splat onto the foul line. But the hand holding the heavy ball had to descend, and when it did, it overbalanced her again. Agnes stumbled forward a few steps with her arms swinging wildly.

At some point during the ungainly display, Agnes inexplicably decided she might as well complete her swing, and she let go of the ball.

Unfortunately, she was turned nearly sideways at the time, and her arm was on an upward trajectory.

She lofted the ball high into the air over the adjoining alley and then put her foot down in the gutter and toppled forward, landing hard with her hands smacking down on the glossy wood of the other team's alley.

All eyes rose to watch the high-arching bowling ball, mouths spreading in horrified "ohs" as it sailed fifteen feet above the lane.

The wrong lane.

The train wreck held them in thrall as the ball completed its upward voyage and started downward, like a lead balloon or a cannonball that had run out of steam.

Agnes's runaway bowling ball finally gave up its flight, slamming to the alley right in front of Devon's ball, to the sound of disbelieving cries all around.

Like an oversized billiard ball, Devon's ball smacked hard into Agnes's errant offering and redirected it down the alley under considerable force.

Everyone came to their feet, barely breathing as the redirected ball shot toward the pins, its line perfectly focused on the head pin. The ball slammed into the pins and sent them flying in a perfect snowplow and dropped triumphantly into the pit.

Agnes had gotten a strike!

Unfortunately, it was on the wrong alley.

The smug young man whose ball had sent hers into the pins was watching his aborted ball slide down the gutter and into the pit without touching a single pin.

There was a startled beat of silence, and then Flo's team leaped off the runway with screams of delight.

Agnes hefted herself out of the gutter as her lowly house ball rolled triumphantly toward her, Devon's fancy ball ambling along on its heels. Roger hurried over and helped her to her feet and gave her a mighty hug as Flo and TC shared a grin across the space between the two teams.

Then Roger left Agnes as the Eagles erupted into screams of outrage. And he and Celia began the hard work of making sure Agnes's strike was counted.

"WE WERE ROBBED," BECAME the battle cry of the Eagles as they all reconvened in the Silver Hills bar an hour later to do a debrief of the event. Agnes had passed the point where she was apologetic for literally waylaying Devon's roll, and had gotten into the spirit of fun both groups decided to embrace.

In his usual diplomatic way, Roger had convinced the Eagles that Flo and Co. would support the Eagles win, as long as the Eagles didn't object to Agnes getting logged as having the strike.

Since everybody liked Agnes, they eventually saw the wisdom in letting her enjoy her moment. Especially since she didn't suffer any illusions about it.

Agnes raised her frosty glass of beer. "To the most unique strike ever struck. I am the reigning queen of weird bowling."

"Here, here!" Everyone shouted, drinking to her Majesty the Weird.

Sitting at a table near the wall with Roger, Flo shook her head, smiling. It was good to see Agnes happy about the outing.

TC came over and tapped her wine glass against Flo's. "To unusual endings."

Flo laughed.

Roger leaned toward TC, lowering his voice. "What did the manager say?"

TC made a face. "They're going to discuss whether we'll be allowed back again. Agnes put a dent in the floor with her lofted ball."

He winced too. "Well, at least no one was hurt this time."

"Well, except for the guy in the next alley who limped away in the beginning," Flo reminded him.

"There is that," Roger agreed. He looked at his empty wine glass and stood. "Can I get you ladies another one?"

"I'm fine," TC said. "I have work tomorrow."

"None for me, hun. But thanks."

Roger touched her shoulder as he moved past and joined the group at the bar. He soon got caught up in the fun there and didn't return to the table right away.

TC slipped into a chair next to Flo. "What's going on with the David Potts investigation? Anything new?"

"I spoke to the youngest son. Peter. He's not happy about his brother's new project."

"I'll bet. Do you think he could have killed his father?"

Flo sipped her wine. Her instinct was to say no. But something about Peter Potts engaged her spidey senses. "I don't think so. But he's apparently got anger issues, so I guess it's possible."

"Anger issues?"

Flo nodded and told TC about her discussion with the young veterinarian.

"That's pretty interesting," TC admitted. "Is there any inkling of a motive there?"

"Not yet." Flo frowned. "I spoke to Vlad and Morty."

"About David Junior's accusation?"

"Yes. Vlad reacted about like you'd expect. But Morty said something interesting. When I asked them if the police would have any concrete evidence that Vlad was at the scene of the murder, she told me to ask Preston Jamison."

"The campaign manager?"

"Yep. She said, and I quote, 'It was his bright idea'. What do you suppose she meant?"

TC shook her head. "No idea. With a political operative, you can't think lowbrow enough. But you know there's only one way to find out, right?"

Flo grinned. "I do know that. I'm going to visit Vlad's campaign headquarters in the morning. Are you up for a visit?"

"I thought you'd never ask!"

THEY SAT IN FLO'S CAR and stared at the storefront on Epoch Street that represented Vlad's campaign headquarters. The sun was just rising behind them, and its glow was doing nothing to make the disreputable space look better.

The sign in the cloudy and streaked window looked like a two-year-old made it with crayons. Vlad's picture was a caricature rather than a photo, and all it was missing was the fangs to make it look like an old promotion for a Dracula film.

"Yikes!" said Agnes, whose weary form was slouching in the back seat. Agnes generally liked to call shotgun, claiming the front passenger seat, but she was dreary-eyed from a long night at the bar with her friends and clutching the biggest coffee they could purchase at the Silver City Coffee House. "It's like he's trying to make himself into a cartoon."

"Maybe their focus groups told them he was too dark and scary so he's trying to make himself less threatening," TC suggested.

Flo grinned. "I have a terrible urge to grab one of those white paint pens and add some fangs."

"Me too," agreed Agnes.

"Why is there nobody here?" TC asked, glancing up and down the street.

Flo glanced at her watch. "It's not quite eight yet. We're a bit early."

"Just a bit?" Agnes grumbled.

Flo glanced in the rearview mirror. "I gave you the option to skip this," she reminded her friend. "You insisted you wanted to come."

"That's because you promised me breakfast." She held her hands up, one of them clutching the enormous coffee, and looked melodramatically around the backseat. "I don't see any breakfast here. Do you?"

Flo and TC shared a look. Agnes was getting crankier by the day. If she didn't happy up soon, Flo was going to sit on her and stuff pie into her face until she smiled.

"There he is," TC said in a whisper.

Sure enough, Preston Jamison had walked up to the scarred and battered front door, which was inexplicably painted an atrocious yellow, and was fitting his key into the lock.

"We're on, ladies." Flo grabbed her purse and slid it over her shoulder as she stepped out of the car, hurrying down the cracked sidewalk. The ugly building consisted of dirty white brick and black, half-rotted timbers. The roof sagged dangerously overhead, a few of the mildewed green shingles puckered at the edge as if they'd been pinched under the thumb of a petulant giant.

A rusty stripe followed the roofline along the sidewalk, stopping in a puddle of orange water near the door.

"Mr. Jamison?"

The campaign manager stopped in the midst of pushing the ugly door inward and looked up, his stance relaxed. "Yes?"

As soon as he saw who'd addressed him, Preston Jamison frowned, his hand tightening on the edge of the ragged door. "Mrs. Bee. Have you come to volunteer for Mr. Newsome?"

Flo barely kept from laughing. "Actually, *Mrs*. Newsome sent me."

Not strictly true, but close enough.

His eyes went hard. "She did, did she? What about?"

Flo stopped just out of range of the dripping, rust-tinged water. TC and Agnes came up behind her, standing on either side like bodyguards.

Jamison's gaze narrowed at the sight.

"She seemed to think you might have compromised Vlad with the police."

He didn't even blink. If he was surprised to hear that Morty disapproved of his actions, he didn't show it. "I can assure you, she's wrong. Now if you'll excuse me..."

"Did you send Vlad to the scene of the murder, Mr. Jamison?"

The surprise on his face seemed genuine. "Why would I do something so ludicrous?"

"Because you didn't know it would be a crime scene at the time?" TC offered reasonably.

"Tell me what you did," Flo demanded.

"I don't have to do what you say," he began.

"Really?" Agnes snorted out. "You're going to use the 'you're not the boss of me' defense?" She shook her head. "I can see why Vlad pays you the big bucks."

Jamison's jaw tightened. His knuckles turned white where he was gripping the door. Finally, he seemed to make an effort to control his temper. He took a deep breath and let the door slide shut. Shoving his hands into his pockets, probably so he wouldn't throttle the three women with them, Jamison inclined his head. "We were at the house the day of the murder. But I can assure you we left no evidence behind."

"Whatever would possess you or Vlad to step into the enemy's territory," Flo asked.

He thought about it for a moment and then sighed. "In retrospect, it was clearly a bad idea."

"Clearly," Agnes agreed.

He spared her a glare before going on. "Our focus groups told us people don't trust rich people. But Potts had done an excellent job of hiding his wealth. He'd come across as one of the little people, just trying to make a living in a tough industry. It was giving him an edge."

"So you thought you'd get a picture of the Potts's house and property," TC speculated.

The campaign manager looked at the ground and nodded. "We did a quick video of Vlad standing in front of the house, talking about how much money the Potts's had."

"What about the industry scandal?" Flo asked. "Why didn't you just use that against him? It seems a lot more salacious than working hard and accumulating a nice living."

"You'd think so. But we got a stronger reaction from the wealth angle. Besides, Potts had the local media in his grip. That scandal was barely covered and it was glossed quickly over."

"You need to go to the police and fess up," Flo told him.

"That's exactly what we *don't* need to do, Mrs. Bee. They have no idea we were there. I don't want to put any ideas in their heads."

"The idea is already there," TC told him. "Trust me, I used to date the detective in charge. He's not going to just overlook David Junior's accusation. Especially since Vlad was the one who stood to gain the most from Potts's death."

Jamison shook his head. "They have no proof. Potts is just flailing around. He's grieving and confused." The campaign manager's expression turned shrewd. "Besides, I'd say Junior has a pretty good motive, himself. Maybe better than Vlad's. He stepped into his father's organization and will probably ride that gravy train all the way to the mayor's mansion."

"And I'm sure Detective Peters will look at him. But, as a person of interest," Flo told him. "Vlad will only look guiltier if they find out you were at the house and you didn't disclose it." Not to mention, Flo was going to have to tell the detective herself if Jamison didn't.

The manager stared at the rusty puddle by his shoe and sighed. "I know, you're right. I just hate putting another road-block in our way."

"Maybe you can spin it somehow," Agnes suggested. "You people are good at that, right?"

He ignored her, clearly not a fan of Agnes's direct, combative style.

Flo threw her friend a look, imploring her with a gaze to take the hostility down a notch.

Jamison seemed to deflate. "Okay. I'll go to them and explain. Show them the video we shot. Hopefully, that will be enough to convince them we weren't up to something devious."

Flo lifted her brows and he clarified. "I mean, a deadly type of devious."

She nodded. "Good. Thanks for listening to me, Mr. Jamison."

He nodded almost absently.

They started back to the car, but he called out to Flo.

She stopped and turned back. "Yes?"

"Maybe it's nothing, but as we were wrapping up, I heard something. A commotion coming from the trees at the side of the property. I left the cameraman and Vlad to finish up and ducked into the woods."

"Did you see the killer?" Flo asked hopefully.

"No."

Of course, it wouldn't be that easy.

"At least, not unless that giant chicken that ran out of the woods killed Potts."

"Giant chicken?" TC asked on a laugh. "Do you have a prescription for medical marijuana, Mr. Jamison?"

Agnes snorted out a laugh as Jamison glared at them.

"I wish," he said with disgust. "As you well know that's not legal in Indiana. And judging by how long it took to get Sunday liquor sales in this state I'm guessing we'll be in the second wave of alien invaders before that becomes law here."

TC chuckled. "You aren't wrong."

"No," Jamison went on. "There's a chicken at Potts's place that's as big as a turkey. The thing's huge. It scared the stuffing out of me, no pun intended, when it came hurtling out of the trees, squawking as if those aliens I mentioned were trying to give it an anal probe with chicken broth."

CHAPTER EIGHTEEN

"REVENGE OF THE GIANT chicken," TC said with amusement in her voice. "I'm totally writing a mystery with that title."

Agnes grumbled unhappily. "Unless this one has S-E-X in it, I'm not reading it, TC."

TC was a mystery writer on the side and on the sly. She wrote her books under the pen name, T. Colombo. The books featured a logo with a TC lookalike wearing a rumpled trench coat and holding a battered notebook, ala the Colombo from the old mystery show.

Though TC and Agnes had a running disagreement about the lack of raciness in TC's books, Flo was privately happy that TC embraced the spirit of a true cozy and kept the books clean and fun. She actually wrote delightful books and was starting to make a name for herself in the online cozy community.

"No sex, Agnes. You know my feelings on that. Besides, for someone who thinks she wants to read racy stuff, you can't even say the word. You always spell it."

"Whatever," Agnes said dismissively, blushing. "That chicken's real, TC," Agnes went on, "Flo and I saw it."

TC's eyes went wide. "Really? Are all his chickens huge?"

Flo shook her head. "I only saw one. And to tell you the truth, it was outside the chicken yard when we saw it. The thing really was monstrous. If I didn't know better, I'd think it had been basted with growth hormones."

"Do you?" TC asked.

Flo slid her a quick look. "Do I what?"

"Do you know better?" When Flo narrowed her gaze, TC clarified. "Isn't it possible Potts was using illegal hormones on his chickens?"

Flo frowned thoughtfully. "I guess that's possible. But if he's slaughtering those amped up birds and selling them for people to eat..."

"People would have a cow," Agnes mumbled without thinking.

TC chuckled. "Yep. That would probably be the end result. After they sued the company into next month. I did some research on this for a book and from what I've read, it takes a lot of hormones to make bigger chickens. They need to get shots like every ninety minutes or so because of their metabolisms. That would be expensive and difficult, but if he'd found a way to shortchange that operation it could be very profitable."

"The public will still get stuck on the whole super-hormones thing," Agnes said. "They wouldn't even care if it was legal."

TC nodded. "Exactly."

Flo thought about what her friends had said for a moment. It was true, if David Potts had been playing fast and loose with poultry hormones, he might be able to make a lot more money selling his chickens, but he was walking a very dangerous line. "He'd never get that past the FDA."

"No. But if he was growing the chickens off-site, there'd be no visible evidence to alert the testers," TC offered.

"They'd still test the meat," Flo argued as she made the turn into a tall, glass and brick building in the Silver City office park.

"Maybe that fancy scientist Potts hired came up with a way to do it that wasn't detectable," Agnes suggested.

Flo parked the car in a visitors slot and turned to her friends. "This is a lot of conjecture. Let's go see if we can get some facts."

The woman at the information desk in the center of the large, open lobby frowned when she saw them again. She shoved a lank strand of dirty blonde hair off her cheek and picked up the phone.

Flo marched right over and stopped in front of the desk, her footsteps echoing around the big space. She stood staring down at the seated receptionist as if to dare her to continue to ignore them. After a moment, the woman hung up and fixed an unhappy glare on Flo. But when she spoke, it wasn't to reject them again as Flo had expected. "Doctor Macintosh can see you now." She slapped three visitor's badges onto the top of her desk and jammed a finger toward the elevators. "Three oh one. She can only give you five minutes. Her time is valuable."

The implication was clear. David Pott's newest scientist's time was valuable, Flo's apparently was not. She gave the woman a wide smile. "Why, thank you. Five minutes will be more than enough." Naturally, she fully intended to stretch that five minutes into ten or fifteen, but she wouldn't tell the snotty receptionist that.

They hurried toward the elevators, and TC stabbed a finger on the *Up* button. "Somebody must have given *her* an earful."

The door slid open and they stepped inside. Agnes hit the button for the third floor. The elevator across the hall dinged, the door starting to slide open as theirs slid shut.

Their favorite police detective stepped out of the other elevator.

Flo had just enough time to register the unhappy expression on Detective Peters' face before the door shut completely.

"It looks like the police think our scientist was involved too," Agnes said.

"Yes," Flo agreed. "It certainly does. I hope Detective grumpy didn't put our scientist so far off her feed she'll clam up on us." Flo sighed unhappily.

TC was notably silent.

Three oh one was at the far end of the hallway from the elevators. A brass sign on the door proclaimed it to be the office of Audrey Macintosh, Ph.D.

Agnes knocked hard enough to rattle the door in its frame. When TC and Flo gave her a look, she shrugged. "I had a surge of adrenaline there. It's gone now."

Flo doubted it.

Never-the-less, it took two more of Agnes's foundation-shaking knocks before the door opened inward, revealing a small, pasty face with oversized light blue eyes. "Yes?"

The woman didn't appear to know why they were there.

Flo offered her hand. "I'm Florence Bee, Doctor Macintosh. These are my associates, Tricia and Agnes. You were expecting us?"

The woman nodded a bit vaguely but made no move to take Flo's hand. It appeared Detective Grumpy had done more than put a damper on her willingness to cooperate. He'd totally ripped her off her moors.

"Are you okay, hun?"

The woman looked to be in her early forties, but she had dark circles under the overlarge eyes and creases on her forehead that seemed too deeply etched for her age. The wrinkles were probably there because she frowned a lot, which she was currently doing as she seemed to search her memory for their purpose there.

Flo decided to help her with that. "Mrs. Potts hired us to help her find her husband's killer."

With Flo's words, the frown disappeared and tears filled the woman's eyes. Her hand shot up to cover her mouth. A soft sob emerged from behind it. "Poor David. I just c-c-can't believe he's g-g-gone."

Flo wondered if the stuttering was an indication of her distress, or if it was normal for her. She nodded. "It's horrible. But it will be worse if his wife is unfairly blamed for the murder. We're hoping you can help us clear her name."

"I don't understand, how can I do that?"

"Do you think we could come into your office?" Flo cast her gaze up and down the halls, hoping the distraught scientist would get the picture. The last thing they needed was for some unscrupulous listener to tell tales about their business there.

"Oh." The woman blinked rapidly, clearing her throat and swiping at the tears sliding down her cheeks. "I'm s-s-sorry. Come in."

She moved into the oversized large office and motioned toward three black leather chairs clustered around a small table in one corner.

TC and Agnes lowered themselves into the chairs. Flo stood next to one and watched the scientist.

Doctor Macintosh didn't sit down. Instead, she paced over to the windows and stood there, staring through the spotless glass with one hand on her throat. She didn't speak for a long moment.

Flo figured she'd probably been standing there when they'd knocked. Judging by the way the other woman immediately sank into her thoughts, Flo could understand why it had taken her so long to come to the door. The window looked out on a carefully nurtured grassy area with concrete benches and strategically placed tree groupings. It was very pretty and probably highly conducive to deep thought.

"The police were just here?" Flo asked, trying to nudge the woman into talking.

"What?" She half turned, giving Flo the expected frown. "Oh. Yes. H-h-horrible people."

Flo glanced at TC and found her looking sad. "They're just doing their jobs."

The woman at the window didn't respond. She continued to stare through the glass, immobile as a statue.

Flo set her purse in the chair and walked over, stopping next to Doctor Macintosh. She gazed out at the pretty landscaping for a moment and then said, "It's lovely here."

The other woman sighed.

"What did the police ask about?" For a long moment, Flo didn't think the scientist would respond. When she finally did, her response was vague. "Strange and d-d-difficult things."

Flo realized she was getting nowhere fast. If the reception-ist held them to their timeline, they were going to be escorted out of the place with nothing to show for their efforts.

She would have to be more blunt. "Doctor Macintosh, did you kill David Potts?"

The woman twitched, her hand dropping from her throat. Her stance turned rigid, but she didn't look Flo in the eye. She seemed uncomfortable doing that in general. "No."

"Do you know who did?"

Her brow furrowed. She hesitated a beat but then gave her head two quick jerks in the negative.

The woman was lying. Flo would stake her entire savings on it. But she just didn't know how to make the scientist talk. Appealing to her humanity where Nanna Potts was concerned hadn't worked. Maybe she could shock her into talking. "Nanna Potts believes that you were having an affair with her husband. That you fought. And that you killed him."

Doctor Macintosh's head jerked around. She fixed Flo with a rage-filled gaze.

Flo fought the urge to take a step back under the cold fury in the woman's eyes. "That's r-r-r-ridiculous!"

"Is it?" Flo asked. "Why would you leave a lucrative job with Chisholm's Chickens to come here? I've heard only good things about Chris Chisholm. He seems to treat his employees well. Yet you took the formula he'd paid you to develop and left him for his biggest competition. Why would you do that if not for love?"

The woman snorted out a laugh. "Have you ever m-m-met David Potts?"

Flo shook her head.

"That e-e-explains it."

"Explains what," Flo asked.

The scientist turned to face Flo, fully engaged in the conversation at last. "How you can ask me such a ridiculous q-q-question. David Potts was a difficult, unp-p-pleasant man. I'm not in the least surprised that someone killed him."

"So, you were lying a minute ago when you pretended to be sad he was killed?" Flo let her anger show in her tone.

The other woman shrugged. "No. I am s-s-sad. David and I had become friends of a sort. N-n-not the kind you'd have dinner or drinks with, or spend any time at all with outside of the office. But we had a c-c-common goal, and that tends to draw people together."

"What goal was that?" TC asked, sitting forward in her chair.

The scientist looked at her as if she'd forgotten the other women were there. Her lips curved upward in a cold smile. "M-m-money of c-c-course. What else is there of any imp-p-portance?"

"The formula you took from Chisolm's?" Flo asked.

Macintosh leaned closer, stabbing a finger with a ragged nail at Flo. "Let's get one thing s-s-straight here. I didn't t-t-take that formula from C-C-Chris. It was my f-f-formula. I had it ninety percent d-d-developed when I went to work-k-k for him. There was no w-w-way I was going to let them k-k-keep it when I left."

"But why make the change?" Agnes asked. "You say it was about money. Couldn't you have struck some kind of deal with Chisholm to make the same kind of money there?"

"Not a ch-ch-chance. That shark of a wife of his was going to m-m-make sure I didn't s-s-see a penny of the millions my formula would bring in. Unfortunately, she snuck some language into the employment c-c-contract I signed, and I wasn't paying c-c-close enough attention. I should have known b-b-better. But I was excited that I was finally going to g-g-get a chance to see if my theories w-w-worked."

"Can they recreate what you did there?" TC asked.

"No. That dunce Wilcox B-B-Brandt couldn't create a way out of a box with four doors."

Flo shook her head. "Wilcox Brandt?"

"The n-n-nutritional scientist who t-t-took over when I left. To say he's lacking in imagination is a near criminal understatement." She smiled bitterly. "He's t-t-terrified Chisholm's going to f-f-fire him once he figures out Will can't fill my shoes and he'll have to go back to the morgue. He even c-c-called me to ask if I'd get him a job here. C-c-can you believe it?"

Flo absolutely could believe it. "Would that be so bad? You've worked together, I presume. He might be useful as a second chair, or string or whatever the scientific equivalent is."

Macintosh shook her head. "That little w-w-weasel would probably just s-s-steal my formula and go running back to Chisholm."

A knock sounded on the door and the receptionist stuck her head in. "I'm sorry Doctor Macintosh, I got tied up or I would have been here sooner."

The scientist gave the woman an unfriendly smile. "Your t-t-timing is fine. We're done here." Her look all but dared Flo to push back at her expulsion.

Flo was willing to take that dare. "Is that giant rooster at David Potts's place part of your research?"

The woman's face paled even more than its usual pasty tint. For a beat, she looked like she was going to grill Flo about what she knew. But she seemed to master her emotions fairly quickly. She stared down her short, slightly pugnacious nose at Flo. "I have n-n-nothing to do with Mr. Potts's private stock. You'll have to ask his wife about that."

Flo held her gaze for a long moment and then smiled. "Thank you so much for your time, Doctor Macintosh."

The woman inclined her head as if she were British royalty and watched them walk away. But she stopped Flo at the door. "Mrs. B-B-Bee?"

"Yes?"

"It would be a m-m-mistake to underestimate Nanna Potts."

"What are you implying?" Flo asked.

"I'll let y-y-you figure that out. Suffice it to say that the woman is not nearly as meek and helpless as she appears. You'd do well to watch your b-b-back around her."

CHAPTER NINETEEN

WHEN THEY GOT BACK to Silver Hills, the spicy aroma of one of Cook's signature lunches filled the air and made Flo's mouth water.

TC had to return to work and Agnes went upstairs to her apartment, allegedly to check on Tolstoy, though the cat had probably either scammed a way out of the apartment already, or was asleep in a ray of sunshine and wanted nothing to do with his owner.

Flo guessed Agnes was really going upstairs in the hopes of running into Hertz Thomson. Hopefully, Agnes would invite the man down to lunch. No doubt Roger would appreciate another man at their table. He was always sadly outnumbered there.

Thinking of Agnes and her cat, Flo had a pang of sadness. She missed her little Rodney and realized the clinic had been supposed to call her early that morning to tell her how he was and when he could come home. She made a mental note to call over to the clinic to ask them when he could come home.

But first, Flo had something she needed to do. And she wasn't looking forward to it. She walked across the lobby toward the dining room, where Elisa Kemp sat alone at one of the tables, reading something on her cell phone.

Flo needed to get the pulse of the rumor mill, to find out if there was anything she needed to head off.

It was rare to find Elisa sitting alone. Her role as rumor queen required her to have her finger on the pulse of everything that was going on at all times. That required a lot of snooping, which required a lot of inserting herself into everybody's activities so she could suck all the news out of every event.

Elisa looked up as Flo approached and her narrow face split in a smile. "Florence Bee. Just the woman I needed to see."

Oh oh!

The only thing Flo could imagine Elisa would be interested in hearing from her was information about Dave Potts's murder. And Flo had no intention of feeding her that information. Not until she'd turned everything she knew over to the police.

"Hello, Elisa. How are you?"

The woman lowered her long-fingered hand over her phone and slid it away so she could place her bony elbows onto the table. "To tell you the truth, I'm at a loss. This place is like a mausoleum today. I can't wait until tonight's televised debate. Watching the vampire try to come off as warm and friendly against that beautiful young boy who's just lost his father should be entertaining."

"Yes, it definitely should be. I was wondering if you'd heard anything about Nanna Potts?"

Elisa frowned. "Like what?"

With Audrey Macintosh's words thrumming through her brain, Flo felt a totally understandable need for some reassurance about her new employer. "Someone I talked to thinks she's hiding something. I got the impression this person thought Nanna might know more about her husband's murder than she's letting on. Do you know her?"

The question was rumor queen code for "what have you heard through the grapevine?".

Elisa frowned. "You know, it's strange. I don't hear much about Mrs. Potts, despite the fact that her husband's running for mayor. Or was..." The pincer-lips compressed, making her look even more like a bug than before. "She keeps a very low profile." Elisa shrugged. "I'm sorry. But I'll look into it and let you know if I find out anything."

"I'd appreciate that." Flo couldn't help wondering if Nanna's staying under the radar was on purpose. Did Nanna Potts have something to hide? If she did, Flo wasn't going to get it from Elisa Kemp. Flo nodded her head toward Elisa's phone. "Is that TC's new novel?"

The other woman sat forward, her eyes sparkling. "It is! I have to say I'm enjoying it very much. That young woman has quite a talent for unraveling a mystery. I'm guessing you taught her everything you know?" Elisa's dark brows peaked and her smile turned predatory.

Flo realized too late that the trap had been sprung. She knew it was futile, but she attempted damage control none-the-less. "Oh no. She had her mad skills before she met me."

"But surely you've been able to share your expertise?"

Flo shook her head. "No point in buttering me up, Elisa. I can't tell you anything about the Potts murder. Mostly because I don't know anything yet. All I have are a bunch of suspects."

Elisa sat back, some of the sparkle leaving her dark gaze. "But surely one of them has a stronger motive than the others?"

Flo frowned. "David Potts was an unlikeable man. It seems like everyone I speak to has a good reason to dislike him. A couple of them might have thought they had reason to do him harm. But to be honest, there's only one person who might be angry enough to kill Potts in such a violent way."

Elisa waited with breathless anticipation. Literally. The gossip-monger didn't seem to be breathing. When Flo didn't reveal the identity of that person, she finally sucked in a breath and leaned closer. "Well, don't keep me waiting, Flo. Who is it?"

"Mrs. Bee!"

Saved by the day manager.

Flo gave Elisa an apologetic smile and stood, turning to find Richard rushing toward her. He looked upset and Flo panicked. She hurried to meet him. "What is it? Is Roger okay?" Flo saw stars as panic swept her. If anything happened to Roger...

"He's fine. He's out by your car right now."

"Oh," Flo glanced through the front windows but couldn't see her car from that angle. "What's going on?"

Richard touched her arm. "I'm sorry. I've called the police."

"The police?" She looked into Richard's blue eyes, so similar to his father's, and was suddenly unable to breathe. "Please tell me it's not Rodney." Despite the fact that her dog should be safely ensconced in the clinic, she was hardwired to worry about him whenever someone looked at her with pity or concern.

Richard's gaze slid away and her heart stopped beating for a second. But when he lifted it to hers again, he spoke in a soothing voice. "He's still at the clinic, isn't he? He should be safe there."

Relief flooded her. Of course, she was being silly. But if it wasn't Roger or Rodney, then what was it? "Richard Attles, just tell me what's wrong before my imagination gives me a heart attack."

Richard put a hand on her arm and started guiding her toward the door. "I'm afraid the vandals have hit your car again."

"Oh no. Not the tires again?"

"Not this time. But I'm afraid it's worse."

Richard held the door for her and she hurried through, her gaze sliding immediately to her small sedan, which she'd parked at the far end of the lot as always so she could get a few extra steps of exercise. Roger stood beside the car, his phone to his ear. When he saw her, he hurriedly ended the call and started forward. "I don't think you should look..."

Anger suddenly found its way through the fog of worry and Flo shook her head, warning Roger off with a lifted hand. "Don't be silly, Roger. I'm not made of glass. What's happened?"

Roger shifted a worried gaze to his son. Richard sighed. "Someone wrote a warning on your car."

Flo hurried past Roger and slipped between her car and the car next to hers. Red liquid dotted the asphalt and was scrawled in large letters over the side of her car. It looked like blood! When Flo saw it, she took a step back, feeling for a moment as if she might pass out.

A small dog would be much easier to kill than a man. Mind your own business!

"He's okay, doll," Roger reassured her quickly. "I just called over to the clinic. Detective Peters is on his way here."

Flo allowed Roger to wrap an arm around her and pull her into his reassuring warmth. Tears slipped down her cheeks and the anger she'd leaned on a moment earlier died behind a wave of real fear. "I have to see him."

Roger nodded. "Of course. We'll take my car."

Flo forced herself to look at the threat one last time before she allowed Roger to lead her away. Rage finally regained a foothold as she thought about the type of person who would do such a thing, and she held onto it.

Anger made her spine stiffen and her head lift again.

Anger would get her through the next few hours. During which she was determined to reveal a killer, before he killed again.

RODNEY LOOKED A LOT better than he had the day before. Flo held onto him so tightly he whined. She had to force herself to loosen her grip. Filled with distrust of the people at the clinic, she found that she was unable to speak to the techs who greeted them and led them to her dog. Thank goodness for Roger. He exuded his usual charm and got them quickly taken back to the visiting rooms and had Rodney brought to Flo.

The first thing Flo had done was demand that Rodney be released to her. Flo was adamant about it. They'd discussed it on the short ride to the clinic. She wanted her little dog with her so she could keep an eye on him. Keep him safe.

Her phone rang as the vet tech left the room to fetch the veterinarian. Roger looked on expectantly as she answered the phone. "Hello?"

"Mrs. Bee? It's Detective Peters. Is your dog okay?"

She closed her eyes, tears sliding down her cheeks at his kindness. "Yes, hun. He's fine. Thank you for asking."

"I'm at the scene now. I thought you'd be relieved to know it's not blood. It was just red paint."

Flo sighed her relief. "Oh. I guess that's good at least."

"I'll try to track the paint. If we're lucky, it will be a type and brand we can use to find the person who threatened you."

"Okay." Flo hugged Rodney tightly, eliciting a grunt from the little dog, and kissed him on the top of his flat head. Her mind swirled with questions. Who would threaten her dog? And why? It was clear the threat came from someone involved in the Potts case. Someone she'd spoken to. Possibly the killer. She realized with a start that Peters was talking to her. "I'm sorry, Detective, could you repeat that?"

"I said, you should probably get the dog out of the clinic. If you'd like, we can keep him down at the station until the threat is passed."

He meant until they found the killer. "That's very kind, Detective. But I'm going to keep him with me."

"I don't want to scare you, Mrs. Bee, but the security at Silver Hills isn't the best. I'm not sure either one of you is safe there."

Flo hated to admit it, but he was right. "I...I'll do something." She didn't know what, exactly, but Flo had friends who could help. As soon as the terror for her dog receded enough for her to think, she'd come up with something.

There was a long moment of silence on the line, during which Flo wondered if the police detective was judging her a fool. But when he finally spoke, she realized he'd probably just been reluctant, given his position with the Silver City PD, to make the suggestion he was about to make.

"Massimo Angonetti could probably help you with that."

He didn't elaborate. He didn't need to. Mass had actually offered them protection once before, when Celia had been in danger too.

Flo had found Massimo to be a kind man, but he was also known to straddle the fine line between legal and not so legal. He mostly managed to stay beyond the long reach of the law, but a couple of times since Flo had known the Angonettis, he'd had to disappear for a bit while the smoke cleared.

"Thanks," she told the detective. "That's a good idea."

"Good. And leave the investigating to me from here on out. Believe it or not, I actually do want you to be safe."

Flo swiped at more tears. "What did you think about Doctor Macintosh?"

"She's not telling the whole truth. But I don't like her for the murder. What about you?"

"I agree she's lying about something. She's not the person she pretends to be, detective. She's not weak in any way."

Flo wouldn't tell him about the woman's warning. Peters didn't need another reason to look at Nanna Potts for the murder. And Flo wouldn't give him one.

Unless she determined it was absolutely necessary. It would help if Nanna had an alibi for his death.

She disconnected as the vet tech returned with Rodney's release paperwork. Flo reluctantly settled the little dog to the floor and took the pen the young girl handed her. Rodney immediately set to work snuffling around the floor looking for food.

"I'm actually going to miss this little guy," the young tech said. She tugged the lid off a glass jar of treats and handed a couple to Rodney.

Flo signed the forms and looked up. "Was there anybody here who seemed interested in Rodney? Anybody besides me?"

The girl frowned. "Not that I can think of, no."

"Would it be possible to get a list of everybody who's worked here since Rodney came in yesterday?" Roger asked her with a kindly smile.

The girl looked surprised. "I'm pretty sure management wouldn't like that. It sounds like an infringement of their privacy."

"Just names," Roger assured her in a gentle tone. "No personal information. I'm afraid little Rodney has been threatened. The police have asked us to get the information while we're here."

At the mention of a threat, the young tech's eyes went round. "Oh no! That's terrible. I can assure you that nobody here would hurt him."

Flo handed her the completed forms and the pen. "I'm sure you're right. But someone threatened to harm him while he was here. That implies they thought they could get to him. If you're right, nobody will even know about the list. But if you're wrong, you might be saving my dog's life."

The girl's frown deepened. Finally, she nodded. "I'll get you a copy of the personnel list."

"Thank you so much," Flo told the girl.

"Anything for Mr. Rodney," she said, finally smiling. "You can pay up at the front desk. Give me ten minutes, and I'll meet you up there with the information."

The girl was true to her word. Fifteen minutes later they were back in Roger's car and Flo was perusing the list. "I don't see any names I recognize," she told Roger. Behind her, in the back seat, snuffling and scratching sounds told Flo Rodney was settling in for a nap.

"What did the Detective say?" Roger asked.

"He wants me to ask Mass for protection."

"That's not a bad idea. I'm sure Celia could help with that."

Flo nodded. "That's what I was thinking. I'll talk to her today." Flo thought about it for a long moment and then turned to Roger. "Would you mind taking a bit of a detour?"

"Of course not, doll. Where to?"

"I think it's time to visit Vlad's competition for mayor."

CHAPTER TWENTY

IN STARK CONTRAST TO Vlad's campaign headquarters, David Potts's place was a hub of activity. He'd taken over a vintage brick building on Main Street and the large picture windows were covered in professionally produced banners showing young David Potts standing with his arm around his father's shoulders.

It was a smart move, reminding people of the connection while giving them reassurance that David Potts Senior wasn't forgotten in the campaign.

"I can't believe how quickly he got those banners replaced," Roger said as he parked a block away at the curb.

"A testament to what you can do with enough money and support," Flo agreed. She turned to Roger. "Would you mind staying with Rodney? I don't want to leave him alone right now."

"Of course, doll. But you be careful in there, okay?"

Flo gave in to the sudden impulse to kiss him on a warm, bristly cheek. When she drew back, she gave him a warm smile. "You're a wonderful man, Roger Attles."

He chuckled softly. "Tell that to all the people I shredded in the courtroom in my heyday."

She shook her head. "I'm sure you ripped very gently."

He was guffawing as she closed the door and headed up the sidewalk.

The walkways were a hotbed of activity around Potts's headquarters. As Flo headed toward the building, she found herself dodging people who were hurrying away with yard signs in their arms and others carrying rolled-up banners she assumed would find their way into diners and shops around town. Most of the workers appeared to be young, brimming with energy and eyes alight with purpose. As Flo approached the door, a pretty twenty-something brunette opened it for her. "Can I help you find someone, ma'am?"

"You sure can, hun. I'd like to speak to David Potts."

The girl frowned and Flo realized she was probably concerned Flo was asking to speak to senior. Which would make her either cray or unaware to the point of ridiculousness. "Junior, of course," she amended.

The girl's frown cleared. "He's speaking to his manager right now. Can he call you later?"

Flo shook her head. "It's about his father. I really need to speak with him now."

"Okay. Let me just go see..." She held the door open and waited while Flo entered in front of her.

The campaign worker motioned toward a line of black plastic chairs against the front wall. "Have a seat. Would you like coffee or tea?"

"No thank you."

"I'll be back in a minute, then."

Flo watched her climb a set of black wrought iron steps affixed to a brick wall on one side of the cramped room. Her gaze rose to a series of windows that showed another office space above. She could make out the familiar features and carefully styled dark hair of David Potts junior. Flo couldn't see who he was talking to, but whoever it was, he didn't look happy.

Flo took a moment to glance around. The space was almost completely filled with old, scarred metal desks. Every desk held a computer of some kind as well as an old fashioned office phone with lots of buttons on the base. If she thought the area outside the headquarters was busy, the space inside was crazy. People sat two to three at a desk, working the phones and discussing the numbers and graphs that were visible on sheets of paper spread between them.

Flo had figured there would be a lot going on behind the scenes of a political campaign, but it was still fascinating to see it at work.

"Ma'am?"

She looked up to find the young girl smiling down at her. "Mr. Potts can see you. Just go on up those stairs there."

"Thank you." Flo managed to maneuver through the chaos and climbed the steps. She knocked on the heavy wood door to Pott's office. A deep voice answered.

"Come on in, Mrs. Bee."

She pushed the door open and stopped, her smile dying on her face. The girl had said he was talking to his campaign manager. But that couldn't be true.

The only other person in the office was David's mother.

Flo blinked in surprise. "Mrs. Potts?"

Nanna stood up and walked over, clasping Flo's hand in a warm grip. "Mrs. Bee. It's so nice to see you again."

"*You're* David's campaign manager?"

"I am." She grinned, looking happier than Flo would expect given the fact her husband had just been brutally murdered.

"I needed someone I could trust," David said, clasping Flo's hand much as his mother had. "It's nice to see you again, Mrs. Bee."

Flo looked up at him, shocked by his height. He had to be eight inches taller than his brother and his father had been. "I'd say you haven't changed a bit, but that would be a lie. You've gotten so tall."

He laughed. "Well, you haven't gotten any taller, but you do look just the same. And that's no lie."

"Well, I haven't gotten any more gullible, young man."

He laughed. "Please, come in. Have a seat. Prissy said you needed to talk to me about my father?"

Flo studiously avoided Nanna's gaze, feeling awkward. She'd been hoping to talk to him about his mother too. "Yes. I'm not sure if you know that your mother hired me to look into your father's murder?"

David nodded. "She told me. I'll be honest, Mrs. Bee. I told her I didn't think it was a good idea. Vladwicke Newsome is a desperate man. Desperate people do terrible things. My father's brutal murder is proof of that."

"Why do you believe Vlad killed your father?"

He peaked perfectly shaped dark brown eyebrows in surprise. "Seriously? I mean, who had more to gain from dad's death than Newsome?"

Flo's mind ticked off the people who had something to gain. Nanna Potts got rid of a husband who was presumably cheating on her and who wasn't a very nice man on top of that. David Junior got a chance to become mayor with minimal expenditure of time and money and an organization that was already humming along. Chris Chisholm got rid of a competitor who seemingly would do anything to win the market. "There are actually quite a few people," Flo told David. She turned and captured Nanna's gaze. "Including your mother."

Nanna held Flo's gaze, her eyes widening only slightly with surprise. She seemed to have been expecting Flo's accusation. Mrs. Potts stared at Flo for a moment and then nodded, acceding Flo's point. "It's true, my husband wasn't very nice to me. He was bossy, domineering, manipulative. And if he wasn't currently having an affair as I suspected, he's had enough of them in the past."

David junior gasped. "Mom. Why didn't you tell me?" He'd clearly had no idea what his mother's life had been like.

She shook her head. "Because I was weak. I shouldn't have let him keep me down." Her eyes gained a pleading quality when she glanced at Flo. "Do you know that I used to be quite a powerful woman?" Flo's surprise must have shown in her face. "It's true. I was the campaign manager for Governor Beckham back in the eighties. I steered him through two successful elections. David and I actually met on a campaign." Her eyes turned dreamy. "We had so much in common back then. Such a passion for making things better in the state. He could be quite charming." She smiled sadly. "But then I married him. And when I got pregnant, he insisted I stay home full time."

David frowned and his mother hurried to reassure him. "I loved every minute of being with you kids. I don't regret a day of it. But you don't need me anymore. You haven't for a long time. And I was chomping at the bit to become useful again."

"Your husband still didn't want you to work?" Flo asked gently.

Nanna shook her head. "I was actually the one who talked him into running for mayor. I stupidly believed that he'd let me be his manager."

"But he didn't," Flo said, understanding how frustrating that must have been for her.

"He laughed at me. Told me I didn't know how things worked anymore." Tears filled her gaze and she blinked them angrily away, smiling at her son. "But I'm here now, and I intend to make sure Davie is the next mayor of Silver City."

In that moment, Flo hoped she did. "You realize the story you just told me makes you a very strong suspect."

She shrugged. "It's all true. I haven't lied to you, Flo. I didn't kill my husband and, despite the fact that David and I were no longer close, I do want you to find out who killed him."

Flo thought about that for a moment and then turned to David Junior. "If I told you Vlad didn't kill your father, who would be your second choice for the murderer?"

He glanced at his mother. For a startled moment, Flo thought he was going to name her. But Nanna inclined her head slightly and he expelled air. "Newsome is the person who stood to gain the most from dad's death. But, if it was a crime of passion, Chris Chisholm had the best *reason* to get rid of my father. He was treated very shabbily by dad. And his business was suffering greatly because of it."

BY THE TIME FLO RETURNED to Roger's car, her dog was sitting on Roger's lap, with his head hanging out the open window, barking at everyone who came within ten feet of the car.

Roger gave her a look filled with relief when she opened the door. "Thank goodness, I was pretty sure someone was going to call the police with a noise complaint soon. I'd say he's feeling better."

Flo laughed and patted her thighs for Rodney to scamper over. He put his fat front paws on her chest and proceeded to give her neck and chin a serious scouring with his long, pink tongue. "Okay, boy. Settle down now. "

Rodney whined once and then turned circles in her lap before sinking down with a happy sigh.

"I guess I know why he was barking now," Roger said. "He missed his mommy."

Flo laughed. "He's hopelessly attached to me, I'm afraid. I'm so sorry, hun."

Roger shrugged. "Don't be. I haven't had so much attention from pretty women for a very long time." He winked. "Even if most of it was of the negative variety."

Flo laughed.

Roger started the big old Cadillac. "Shall we get some lunch?"

"If you don't mind, I'd like to make one last stop before we eat. Can you hold on for a bit longer?"

"I'm all yours. Where to?"

"Chisholm's Chickens. I need to speak to Chris Chisolm about a murder."

CHAPTER TWENTY-ONE

THE OFFICES FOR CHISHOLM'S Chickens was vastly different from the Potts Farms offices. Where Potts Farms had been cold and sterile, like a rented business space, Chisholm's Chickens operated out of a tall, slender building on the edge of town, four levels of red brick with black wrought iron embellishments and a flat roof with a garden area surrounded by wrought iron fencing.

A few young people with weary expressions and greasy hair wandered back and forth on the street in front of the building. They were dressed in clothes that looked as if they hadn't been washed in several days and were holding signs that showed headless chickens lying in pools of blood. If the gory drawings weren't enough, they were chanting, "Murder isn't just for people. Stop the slaughter!"

Flo was tempted to stop and talk to the activists, even catching the eye of one young woman with hair so pale it was almost white. But Roger took her arm and led her away from the group toward the front door.

"Roger?"

"Let Peters deal with that group, doll. That's not part of your investigation."

"It might be. How will I know if I don't talk to them?"

"Because if they'd killed David Potts, they'd be long gone."

"Or they're hanging around to kill the Chisholms too," she said.

"Let the Detective handle it," Roger said with heat in his voice.

Flo had never heard him speak that way. It was a testament to how frightened he was for her. She finally nodded, telling herself she could always come back later to talk to them if she thought it was warranted.

Roger opened the door and ushered her through with an apologetic smile. Flo placed a hand on his face to let him know she understood.

The interior was done up in country chic, with fun chicken and rooster art on the walls and clustered in quirky groups around the room. The floor was covered in charcoal grey carpet with red, yellow and aqua swirls and the waiting area was situated around a large screen television playing old Bugs Bunny and Road Runner cartoons, featuring Foghorn Leghorn.

Flo pointed to the television as they walked through the door.

Roger chuckled. "That used to be my daughter's favorite cartoon."

Flo nodded. "My son loved it too. Kids today have to watch educational cartoons. Some of them are just weird."

He nodded. "I know. I sat through a couple of hours of some pretty uninspiring dreck with my great-grandson last week. I guess there must be some science behind it though. The kid seemed to respond."

Flo shook her head. "Give me some good old slapstick and a giant, mouthy chicken any day."

Roger winked. "Kind of like hanging out with Agnes, eh doll?"

"Can I help you?"

Flo jumped in surprise. She hadn't seen the woman tucked away behind a black desk in the corner. Rodney squiggled in her arms and growled softly as the woman stood up and came out from behind her desk. She was smiling until the little dog curled his lip at her. Then she glowered at him. "You can't bring that dog in here."

Flo opened her mouth to plead her case but Roger beat her to it. "I'm afraid he needs to go where she goes. He's her emotional support dog."

The woman looked at Rodney, whose little lip quivered above his teeth as he told her exactly what he thought of her. She frowned. "He's kind of hostile for an emotional support pet, isn't he?"

Flo shushed him. "He's just very protective. As long as I'm holding him, he's—er—I'm fine."

The woman didn't look convinced. Fortunately, she appeared to be politically correct enough not to want to push the issue. "What can I help you with?"

"We're here to speak with Mr. Chisholm."

"Did you have an appointment?"

"No," Roger interjected smoothly. He moved forward, offering the woman his hand. "I'm Roger Attles, of *Janick, Attles and Benedick*. I'm here to discuss a legal matter with Mr. Chisholm."

Flo watched the forty-something woman with bright green eyes and a shiny fall of smooth auburn hair succumb to Roger's considerable charm. She smiled, letting him clasp her hand in his. "I'll just see if he's available to chat."

"Thank you so much, dear," Roger said.

When he turned back to Flo and grinned, she rolled her eyes, fighting a smile. "You're incorrigible, Mr. Attles," she whispered.

"Isn't that what you like about me, doll?"

Flo thought about it for a beat and then nodded. "It's definitely one of my favorite things," she finally admitted.

His chuckle rumbled pleasantly between them.

"Mr. Chisholm has agreed to speak with you," the receptionist said in a chirpy voice. "Follow me, please."

RODNEY BARKED AS THEY came through the door into Chisholm's office. He growled low in his throat and all the hair on his back stood at attention. But he wasn't looking at the man seated behind the big white desk, his gaze was locked onto the black-haired woman with the deep-burgundy lips, who was sitting near the window. Her long legs were crossed at the knees and she held a folder bearing the Chisholm logo on the front—two interlocked C's with a chicken feather as an exclamation point.

The receptionist stayed several feet away from Rodney, frowning at Flo. "Mr. Chisholm, this is Mr. Attles and Ms...?"

"Florence Bee," Flo said, walking over to offer her hand to the owner and CEO of Chisholm's as he stood.

Rodney kept his eye on the woman across the room. A growl still throbbed in his tiny chest, despite Flo's efforts to shush him.

Chisholm narrowed deep-set hazel eyes. He glanced at Flo's hand and then at Rodney and gave her a wary smile. "Sorry. It seems being polite in this instance might be hazardous to my health."

Flo dropped her hand. "I apologize. He's been ill. I'm afraid he's feeling a little cranky at the moment." What she didn't tell them was that her little man was pretty much cranky all the time, with everybody who wasn't her.

Roger shook Chris Chisholm's hand. "Roger Attles. It's a pleasure to meet you, Mr. Chisholm."

Chisholm didn't look surprised to see a lawyer standing in his office. "Did Arthur fill you in?"

Flo blinked in surprise. Arthur? Roger's old partner? She glanced toward Roger as he nodded. "I can assure you that, *Janick, Attles and Benedick* are doing everything they can to find a satisfactory solution to your problem."

Flo frowned, suddenly feeling as if Roger had pulled one over on her. She didn't like the feeling. Not one little bit. And it was so out of character for Roger. "Excuse me...?"

Roger glanced her way and his expression turned apologetic. "I'm so sorry, Mrs. Bee." He turned to Chisholm. "I'm actually here for an entirely different matter, Mr. Chisholm. David Pott's widow has asked Mrs. Bee to look into his murder. She has a few questions for you."

Chisholm scratched the sparse blond hair on top of his triangular head, looking flummoxed. "But I thought you were here to discuss my case."

"I'm confident that Arthur has it well in hand."

"I don't know what the problem is," the woman across the room barked out in an uncompromising tone. "Potts is dead. Unless his widow is going to follow in his treacherous footsteps, the legal situation should be—malleable," she said with a sneer.

Roger gave her a tight smile. "Mrs. Chisholm?"

She nodded.

Roger didn't offer to shake her hand, a breach in decorum that was so much outside Roger Attles's usual code of conduct that it spoke volumes on his opinion of the woman.

"The estate hasn't been settled yet. The will hasn't even been read. These things take time to sort out."

"I'll sort it out in one afternoon," the sneering woman barked. "I'll invite Nanna to the club for lunch and golf. We'll come to an agreement in a fraction of the time it will take you high-priced lawyers."

Roger's stance stiffened slightly, but he laughed. "I'm sure you will."

Flo thought it might be a good time to step in. "Mr. Chisholm, I was wondering if you had any insight into who might have wanted David Potts dead?"

The odious woman by the window laughed heartily. "Who *wouldn't* want him dead? That list would be much shorter."

Chisholm gave his wife a quelling look. It bounced off her like water off a sizzling hot pan. "What my wife is trying to say..."

"Don't do that, Chris! Don't rewrite my words. I hate that."

Flo thought that maybe Mrs. Chisolm hated a lot of things.

"What I was going to say was…" he went on with a glare toward his wife, "—that Potts wasn't a well-liked man. He'd become even less pleasant in recent years, as he ran his once thriving business into the ground and became desperate."

"Desperate enough to steal a valued employee out from under you?" Flo suggested.

Chisholm's thin lips compressed. "I don't care about the employee, Mrs. Bee. Ms. Macintosh wasn't loyal. I don't keep people around me who aren't loyal."

"A-A-Audrey wasn't nearly as s-s-smart as she thought she was," Mrs. Chisholm said, meanly. "We'll be fine without her."

Flo nodded. "I understand you've replaced her already. With a Mr. Brandt?"

Chisholm nodded enthusiastically, tugging on an oversized ear. "Wilcox isn't as innovative as Audrey was, of course. But he's already making his mark. He's come up with something that's sure to help us leapfrog Potts Farms, even with the formula Audrey stole from us."

"Oh?" Roger asked with an interested smile. "Is it something you can share?"

When Chisholm skimmed him a narrow-eyed look, Roger shrugged, his demeanor exuding harmless interest. "I'm a bit of a business nerd," he said. "I'm interested in the art of competition."

"Brandt's come up with a way to make the chickens much larger," Mrs. Chisholm barked out. "It's revolutionary."

Flo fought to keep her expression neutral. "That's—fascinating."

"Yes," Chisholm said, giving her a slightly vague look. "It is, isn't it? I'm very pleased he was able to come up with something so promising after Audrey deserted us. And so quickly too."

Very quickly, Flo thought. One might say, too quickly. "Mr. and Mrs. Chisholm, have you had any trouble with the activists outside?" Flo asked.

"Trouble?" Mr. Chisholm frowned. "Other than them getting in my face screaming at me every time I come to work?" He grimaced. "Nasty group. I'll be glad when they lose interest and move on."

Flo felt Roger's gaze on her but didn't allow him to catch her eye. "They've apparently moved on from the Potts's residence since David Potts's death." She slid a look to Mrs. Chisholm and saw the woman smirk before she mastered the emotion. "Does that seem suspicious to you?"

Mrs. Chisholm shrugged. "Who knows what goes through those people's minds. They're just bullies. If you get in their faces they back right down."

It takes a bully to know a bully, Flo mused. "So you're not worried about them?"

"No." Chisholm didn't hesitate. He glanced at his wife and they shared a smile. "We're both armed at all times. If one of those whackadoodles comes after us, they'll be on the losing end of the confrontation."

Flo felt all the color leave her face. She finally slid Roger a look. He let his eyes widen slightly in silent communication. Then he stood, offering Chisholm his hand again. "Thank you for seeing us, Mr. Chisholm. Good luck with your new project."

Flo expressed the necessary niceties and led Roger out of the office, her mind swimming with new information, fresh concerns, and one burning question.

If it was true that the "revolutionary" larger chicken was Wilcox Brandt's handiwork, then how had it ended up at David Potts's private residence?

THEY DROPPED RODNEY back at Silver Hills after extracting a promise from Agnes that she'd sit in the apartment with him. Just in case.

Still, Flo was nervous about her little dog as they sat down in a booth at the Silver City Diner. She made a quick call to Celia and asked if she'd talk to Mass about getting a man over to the apartment to keep an eye on Rodney and Agnes. Ce promised there would be someone there when Flo returned home. Feeling better, Flo disconnected and refocused her thoughts on lunch and their recent visit to the Chisholms.

"You threw me for a bit of a loop over the Arthur thing," she gently chastised Roger.

He nodded, leaning away from the table as the waitress settled their salads in front of them. When she was gone, he smiled. "I am sorry, doll. It was a spur of the moment decision. I knew Arthur was representing them and thought it might be a good way to get in the door."

She nodded. "Well, it worked beautifully."

He poured dressing over his salad. "It did."

"Unfortunately, I came away from that interview with more questions than answers."

"Such as what?" he asked, spearing a cherry tomato.

"Such as, if Wilcox Brandt created the giant chicken, what was it doing at Potts's house?"

"Maybe Chisholm brought the chicken over to taunt Potts with," Roger offered.

Flo nodded, swallowing a bite of salad. "That's certainly possible. But if that's the case, why would he leave the chicken there? It just points to him being there when Potts was killed. Along with a pretty good motive for murder, any reasonable person would consider him the strongest suspect."

"Maybe the chicken got away from him. It could have gotten startled when he murdered Potts."

"I guess so. There were a lot of chicken feathers around the site." Flo winced, remembering the gory scene. "I wonder if they can do forensics on a chicken feather to see which chicken it came from."

Roger laughed. "Chicken DNA? I'm sure it's possible."

Something was nagging at Flo, but she couldn't quite grasp it.

"Would you like some pie, doll?"

She dragged herself from her thoughts and shook her head. "No. But thank you, hun. This was just what I needed."

"You didn't eat much."

"I wasn't all that hungry. This case has my stomach twisted in knots."

Roger sat back, his fingers wrapped around a tall glass of iced tea. "Murder is such an ugly business. And this murder was gruesome."

Flo nodded. She was staring at her phone, thinking.

"Penny for your thoughts."

Flo's gaze jerked to Roger's and she sighed. "I need to talk to Wilcox Brandt."

"Whatever for?"

"I'd like his assessment of Doctor Macintosh. It's poor investigative work to only get her side of things. He's surely got an interesting perspective. If he actually did come up with a method for creating a giant chicken, he's not as feeble or dumb as she implied. That makes me wonder what else she told me that wasn't true."

"Good point. Shall we go back to Chisholm's?"

She thought about his suggestion for a moment, not liking the idea of facing off with Chris Chisholm and the dragon he called wife again. "I wish I could talk to him outside of the lab environment. I can't help feeling that we would have had a better interview with Doctor Macintosh if we hadn't been on her turf."

"There's something to be said for that." Roger thought about it for a moment and then pulled out his cell phone.

"Who are you calling?"

He punched some keys and then put the phone to his ear before responding. "I'm calling Mr. Brandt. We might as well just ask him straight out if he'll meet us."

Flo had a face-palm moment. "You're such a smart man," she told him smiling.

To Flo's vast surprise, Roger was put right through to Brandt and, a moment later he was speaking with the man. It only took him a few moments and the promise of a free lunch to talk the scientist into coming to meet them.

Flo allowed Roger to order her pie and coffee, figuring they'd be waiting a while anyway. The Chisholm's Chickens offices were fifteen minutes away without traffic. And, despite the early afternoon hour, the lunch traffic was still bustling.

To her vast surprise, when the man came through the door, Flo recognized him. He limped toward their table when Roger hailed him, eyeing Flo warily.

Flo leaned close to Roger, whispering, "That's the man Agnes hit with the bowling ball. The one who left without threatening to sue."

Roger's eyes widened as, presumably, he recognized the other man. "I believe you're right, doll."

Roger stood up and offered Brandt his hand. "Mr. Brandt. Thank you so much for meeting with us." He motioned toward an empty chair. "Please, sit down. Shall I call the waitress over?"

Brandt skimmed Flo a look that could only be described as hostile. "Not just yet. I'll eat after we're done talking."

In other words, he wanted to eat alone.

Flo quickly assessed the scientist. He looked to be in his early forties, with thick, wavy light brown hair that he wore long enough to brush his jawline. The hair hung from a center part and obscured a large portion of his face. Wary brown eyes peered out from between the curtain of hair, and his lips were compressed from something that looked a lot like anger. But she couldn't imagine what she or Roger had done to make him mad.

"Mr. Brandt, I want to apologize for what happened at the *Bounce & Bowl* last night. My friend is just learning to bowl. It hasn't been a smooth learning experience."

His mouth opened and he peered at Flo with obvious surprise. "That's what this is about?" He seemed to relax. "I saw you at the office today and thought you were with the FDA."

What a strange conclusion for him to jump to. Neither Flo nor Roger looked anything like FDA agents. For one thing, they carried a bit too much gray around on their heads for the job.

She tried a carefree laugh but his gaze narrowed at the attempt. "Not FDA, no. But it is a small world, isn't it? I'm actually looking into David Potts's murder."

She watched him carefully, expecting a reaction from the news.

He seemed totally uninterested. "Oh. Well, I've never met the man so I don't know how I can help you."

"Actually, I wanted to ask you about Audrey Macintosh."

That brought about a reaction. Brandt jerked as if struck and straightened his rounded shoulders. His lips compressed again, the bottom one sticking out just slightly. He looked like a petulant child. "I have nothing to say about Audrey."

"I know she didn't leave under the best of circumstances," Flo said.

Brandt gave a bitter laugh. "That's the understatement of the century. She created a mess and then walked away, leaving me to clean it up."

Roger rested his forearms on the table, clasping his hands. He searched Brandt's face with an earnest look. "That must have made you very angry."

"Angry? Please, I'm drowning in understatement here. The woman's an evil hag. I hope she goes to prison."

"Prison?" Flo asked. "For taking the flavoring formula?"

"*Stealing* the formula, you mean."

"She says it was her formula. She developed it before coming to Chisholm's."

"But she signed away the rights to it. The patent was filed in the company name. It belonged to Chisholm. Besides, I wasn't talking about that. I meant for killing Potts."

Flo wasn't able to hide her surprise. "You believe she killed him? Why? From what she told us, she viewed him as her ticket to money and fame."

Brandt scoffed. "That sounds like her. I didn't know Potts, but I knew of him. All of us at Chisholm's did. He was a jerk, single-minded in his pursuit of his own advancement. The two of them were destined to clash. It was only a matter of time. I'm only surprised it happened so quickly."

"Mrs. Potts believed they were having an affair," Flo said, just to gauge his reaction.

Something moved quickly through Brandt's gaze. It looked like pain. "It's very possible. Audrey would do anything to get what she wanted."

"You said Audrey left you to clean up her mess," Roger said. "What did you mean by that?"

"Look, I'm not a stupid guy, but I know my limitations. As much as I hate her for what she did, I'm man enough to admit she was a rock star in the lab. Audrey had a creative scientific mind. A very rare combination. She was always looking for creative ways to use old ideas to get new and better results.

I learned a lot from her. But I was just Audrey's assistant. When she left, the Chisholms looked to me to produce like she had." He shook his head, his lips pursing. "I'm just not that guy."

"But they said you'd already come up with a way to grow extra-large birds," Flo said encouragingly.

He shrugged. "I'd managed to grow one giant bird. But the pressure was on for me to grow a second. For some reason, I couldn't duplicate my efforts. I went to Audrey and asked her for help. She laughed at me."

Flo wasn't surprised. Audrey Macintosh wouldn't win any awards for humanitarian of the year, but her instincts were attuned to her industry. She was on the cusp of blowing Chisholm's out of the water with her formula. It would be self-defeating to help Brandt find a way to succeed. "You can't really blame her, can you?" she asked gently.

The man blinked, but not before Flo saw pain slide through his eyes again. He'd been in love with Audrey Macintosh. Flo would bet her life on it. And Audrey's leaving had done him in emotionally. Then she'd stomped on his heart one more time when he'd asked for help.

"I hope things get easier," she told him gently.

Brandt contracted right before her eyes, folding in on himself. He rounded his shoulders as if to protect his heart. "I have nothing more to say. Please leave now."

Roger and Flo shared a look and then stood.

"Thanks again for seeing us," Flo said.

The scientist buried his nose in the menu, ignoring her.

Roger paid their check and told the waitress to bill him for whatever Brandt ordered too. And then they headed back to Silver Hills.

CHAPTER TWENTY-TWO

FLO'S PHONE RANG AND she grabbed it, hitting the button when she saw Agnes's name on the screen. "Hi, hun. I'm heading back now."

"Ce's guy is here."

"Oh good," Flo said, relief filling her.

"Ce also wanted me to tell you that her friend Andy can see us in twenty minutes."

Flo frowned, trying to make sense of what Agnes was telling her. Then she remembered. Andy was Celia's friend the pathologist. "Oh, that's great news. Roger and I are two minutes away, we'll pick you up out front."

"Whatever you're planning, I can't go with," Roger told her when she'd hung up. "I'm a fourth for Bridge this afternoon. But you can take my car if you want."

"Oh Roger, thank you. Are you sure you don't mind?"

"Not even a little bit," he assured her, clasping her hand and settling a gentle kiss on the palm. "Now tell me what you and Agnes are up to."

ANDY WAS WAITING FOR them outside the Emergency room of Silver City Hospital.

Celia's friend was a big woman. She was about Agnes's size, so Flo guessed her to be close to six feet and well over two hundred pounds.

The pathologist had a pretty face and curly, dark brown hair without a spec of gray in it. She wore the expected white lab coat and, underneath, a clean pair of light green scrubs.

"Hello, Andy," Flo said. She quickly introduced herself, TC, and Agnes.

Andy shook each of their hands. "Celia's told me all about you." She winked at Agnes. "Especially you, Agnes."

"We really appreciate your help," Flo quickly said before Agnes had a chance to wonder why she'd been singled out.

Andy shrugged broad shoulders. "I'm not sure I'll be much help, but I'm glad to talk to you. The cause of death is pretty obvious." Andy pointed to the hard, plastic seating in the waiting room. "Would you like to sit?"

"I was hoping we could see the—you know—bodies," Agnes said hopefully.

TC grimaced. "No bodies for me. But I wouldn't mind seeing the morgue."

"TC's a mystery writer," Agnes said, proudly.

"But she won't read my books because there's no S-E-X," TC teased.

"I read them!" Agnes declared before she caught herself.

TC beamed. "You do?"

"Of course," though Agnes looked like she'd rather eat nails than admit it. "They're pretty good."

"They're excellent books," Flo said, giving TC a smile. "I've read every one of them."

Andy looked genuinely interested. "Oh, what name do you write under? I love mysteries!"

They talked favorite authors for a moment, until Agnes reminded Ce's friend none too subtly that they wanted to see the morgue.

"Okay, but we'll have to make it quick," Andy said. "My boss is at lunch right now. He doesn't like outsiders in the morgue." She led them through a pair of doors to an elevator, stabbing a large finger on the button to go down.

"What about when families come to identify their loved ones," TC asked.

"We have a special room for that, with a window overlooking the main morgue. That doesn't happen as often as you might think."

"Especially not here, in Silver City. Everybody seems to know everybody else," TC agreed.

"Well, actually, you'd be surprised. We get our share of homeless people and illegals who don't carry ID on them," Andy said.

They exited the elevator and headed down a hallway with scuffed linoleum flooring and ugly green paint covering concrete block walls. The fluorescent lighting above their heads was yellowed and dimming, one of them flickering as if ready to go out.

"I'm surprised it doesn't smell," Agnes said.

Andy stopped in front of a pair of stainless steel swinging doors. The small white sign next to the doors read, *Morgue* in black letters. "No smells. All of the bodies are refrigerated."

She pushed the doors open and movement-sensing lights flickered on, illuminating a large room with concrete floors and a continuation of the concrete block walls. In bright contrast to the ugly hallway, the walls in the morgue had been painted a lively, clean white.

The area on the end farthest from the door consisted of two long rows of stainless steel, refrigerator-type doors. Andy saw the direction Flo was looking and inclined her head toward them. "That's where we keep the bodies."

"Are they all full?" Agnes asked, taking a step in that direction.

"Only about half of them are occupied right now. That's actually more than we usually have in here."

"Can I wander around?" TC asked, her expression filled with interest.

"Of course. Just don't touch anything."

Agnes followed TC toward a couple of stainless steel autopsy tables and Flo said a little prayer that her friend would honor Andy's wishes and not touch them.

Heaven knew Agnes never listened to Flo or anybody else.

What she needed was to get her friend a giant red "No!" button.

"Can you tell me anything about David Potts's body?" Flo asked. "Aside from the obvious? Like, had he been drugged?"

"We didn't find any drugs in his system and no evidence of recreational drug use. There was also no alcohol. But his stomach contents told us he was a fan of Indian food," Andy said, smiling. "You might be interested to know that he was already dead when he was decapitated."

Flo's eyes went wide. "Really? That is interesting. What killed him?"

"His skull was cracked. He was bludgeoned with something wide and curved."

"Like a shovel?" Flo remembered the shovel she'd seen in the storage area of the coop. The memory triggered a jolt of panic. What if she and Agnes had manhandled the murder weapon? Detective Peters would have a stroke.

"Maybe, but I'm thinking it was something smaller than that."

Relief flooded her. "Oh, okay. Anything else?"

"A couple of chicken feathers in his mouth, which might have happened during a struggle with his killer."

"Could they have been put there on purpose, as a message? For example, from someone who hated the slaughter of chickens for food?"

"Like a radical vegan? Possibly. Do you know someone like that?"

"Some animal rights activists have been in that area recently."

Andy nodded. "I'm afraid that's all I have."

Her cell dinged and she glanced at the text she'd apparently received. "I have to get back to the lab." She glanced toward Agnes, who had her head under a stainless steel table across the room and was apparently trying to see where the drain led. Andy lifted her phone, addressing Flo. "This is time sensitive. Do you think you could see yourselves out?"

"Absolutely. I'll go round up the girls."

"Thanks, Flo." She spun on her heel and hurried from the morgue, closing the door quietly behind her.

Flo watched the pathologist hurry out and then turned back to her friends. "We need to go."

"Five more minutes?" TC pleaded. "I'm getting such great information." She lifted her phone and snapped some pictures of the tools set up neatly on top of a rolling cart.

Apparently bored with the autopsy tables, Agnes wandered away.

TC was busily typing notes into her phone, her gaze wide with excitement. Flo didn't have the heart to disappoint her. "Five minutes, then we really need to g…"

All the lights in the room went out with a loud snap.

Silence pulsed around them. Over to the side of the room, where Agnes had gone, there was a loud thump and the sound of something rolling across the floor.

"Agnes? Are you okay?"

Nothing.

"Agnes?"

A loud clatter announced TC's attempt to move. "Flo? I can't see anything. It's pitch black in here."

Unfortunately, the morgue was underground and there were no windows to ease the dark.

"I'm sure there's some kind of generator that will kick on soon. We should just stand still until it does." But Flo was concerned by Agnes's silence. "Agnes, talk to me, hun. You're worrying me."

A heartfelt groan eased through the darkness. Flo's pulse spiked with fear. "I think Agnes is hurt, TC."

"I'd go see but, wait a minute." There were fumbling noises, then the sound of something clanging into stainless steel. "Dangit!" TC hissed. "Ouch!"

"What? What are you doing?" Flo took a tentative step forward but her hip banged against something and she stopped, rubbing the sore spot. That was going to leave a bruise.

"I dropped my phone. Hold on." A soft light finally came on, illuminating TC's worried face. She used the phone to move across the space to Flo. "Come on we'll..." The screen light went out. TC fumbled with it until it came on again. She looped her arm through Flo's. "We'll find Agnes and, if she's hurt, I'll use my phone to get out of here and get help."

Flo nodded, wishing she hadn't left her own cell phone in Roger's car.

They started across the space toward where they'd last heard Agnes. It was somewhere over near the drawers. Flo had a sudden horrifying thought. "TC, what if Agnes opened up one of those refrigerated drawers?"

TC expelled air. "And fell inside? I wouldn't even be surprised."

Flo wouldn't either. She just hoped her friend hadn't hit her head in the process. TC shone her light over the area in front of the long line of refrigerated drawers. The light skimmed like a ghostly entity over the surface of the stainless steel.

No Agnes.

"Where could she have gone?" TC asked in a whisper.

"Why are you whispering?" Flo asked.

A soft click sounded across the room.

Flo and TC stilled. TC's arm tightened against Flo's side. Her friend leaned in. "Did that sound like a door being locked?" she whispered.

That time Flo didn't question her whispering.

Flo nodded, then glanced down at the light, realizing it was illuminating them while the darkness hid whoever had just locked the door. She laid her hand over the screen, blocking the light, and whispered back, "We're not alone in here. I'm thinking the lights going out wasn't an accident."

Which meant nobody would be coming to help them.

TC clasped Flo's arm, sliding her hand downward, and then pressed the comforting rectangle of her phone into Flo's hand. "Stay here, don't move," she whispered.

Before Flo could stop her, she was gone.

Flo strained to hear where TC had gone, intending to follow. But her friend moved so quietly Flo only occasionally heard the soft scuff of her sneakers against the concrete floor as she moved into the darkness.

Flo clutched the phone, feeling vulnerable standing there in the darkness. Her only comfort was that the person stalking them would be just as blinded as they were.

Or would he?

Flo started backing up, using the brief view of the area illuminated in TC's sweep of the space to guide her steps. She bumped up against something heavy that rolled slightly and she jolted to a stop. Running her hand along the surface, Flo found a cool, smooth edge that told her it was a table.

She started working her way around the table, grimacing when her fingers touched a slippery wetness that she hoped wasn't blood. Then her hand touched a moist, rubbery surface and she yelped, jumping backward.

Footsteps lurched in her direction, and Flo barely had time to duck behind the table as something swished through the air, inches from her face. She hit the ground hard, her knees screaming upon impact, and scrabbled around the table, getting as far underneath it as she could.

Flo bumped into a lighter-weight cart and it rolled away from her, clanging loudly as it hit the wall.

The footsteps pounded in her direction again. Flo covered her mouth to keep from crying out as something banged into the table above her head.

Flo kicked out, her shoe connecting with a bony limb and eliciting a cry of pain from her attacker.

She dove under the table, crawling out the other side as soft cursing filled the air behind her.

Across the room, a muted whooshing sound preceded the opening of one of the drawers. A gentle light filled the space above the gray, mottled form of a dead woman, whose belly rounded the paper shroud covering her.

The footsteps on the other side of the table started off in that direction, and Flo wondered how their stalker could see where he or she was going. There was only one answer. It had to be someone who knew the morgue very well.

She watched the person move over and peer around the open drawer. With the soft light of the drawer behind him, all Flo could make out was the silhouette of a large form.

While their attacker was busy by the drawers, Flo risked hitting the button on the phone and engaging the lighted screen. She quickly held it up, scanning her surroundings for something she could use to fend him off if he came back.

She caught sight of movement over by the door and jumped to her feet as TC's familiar form appeared. Using the light to guide her, Flo took off running just as TC turned.

"Look out, Flo!"

That was when she heard the footsteps pounding toward her from behind.

She didn't have time to react. Something hit her hard, plowing into her like a freight train and sending her flying.

She smashed hard into the unforgiving floor, and her assailant landed on top of her. Agony tore through her as her ribs were crunched beneath the much heavier weight.

TC's phone clattered to the floor above Flo's head. To Flo's horror, the light on the phone illuminated a thick arm lifting out to the side, a scalpel clutched in meaty fingers.

The killer was going to use the knife on her!

She cried out and tried to shift her attacker's weight, but gained only a breath-stealing jolt of pain for her efforts.

TC's sneakers slapped toward them across the space. She let loose a nerve-rattling scream as she swung her arm, hitting Flo's attacker with something that clanged loudly through the silence as it connected with a skull. The assailant sagged down to the floor, still half covering Flo.

The knife hit the floor and skidded away.

Flo rested her forehead on the cool concrete as nausea swept through her. She was terrified and couldn't breathe from the weight pressing her into the hard floor, and the pain spiking through her ribs.

"Oh my goodness, Flo! Are you okay?" TC grabbed at the thick arms splayed out over the floor and tugged, somehow managing to roll Flo's attacker off after much grunting and tugging.

Flo helped as much as she could, and was relieved when the dead weight finally rolled off, a beefy hand smacking loudly against the floor as it landed.

"I hope that hurt," TC mumbled.

Flo engaged the light on the phone again and allowed TC to help her roll over too. "Is he...?"

TC's pretty face was fixed in a scowl, looking downright murderous in the weak light. "He's unconscious. Hopefully I gave him a concussion."

Flo's eyes widened. "Agnes!"

"I'm okay," a rusty voice said. TC grabbed her cell and turned the light toward the sound of Agnes's voice. She was sitting up on the table Flo had been hiding beneath, a thin trickle of blood running down her face. "Somebody hit me in the head."

Fortunately, Agnes's head was very hard.

Still, her friend looked too pale. TC glanced toward the dark mound on the floor a few feet away from Flo. "We need to get out of here."

Flo nodded and pushed slowly to her feet. Invisible blades were jabbing into her chest and she nearly passed out as she gained her feet. TC grabbed her under one arm and Agnes put a heavy arm around her waist. Between them, they started her across the floor.

They almost made it too. But the sound of a safety being clicked off drew them to an abrupt halt.

A moment later, a flashlight beam cut the distance between them and the killer. "I don't think so, ladies."

The voice was familiar. Flo had heard it before. Recently. But with pain zigzagging through her torso, she was having trouble remembering where. They turned slowly but could see nothing but an amorphous shape behind the bright light.

"You three are not leaving this morgue," the voice said. "At least, not on two legs."

"What is your deal?" Agnes asked. "I haven't done anything to you. Unless..." She thought for a moment and then frowned, narrowing her gaze. "Devon?"

Flo rolled her eyes. "I'm pretty sure we're not about to be killed over a bowling accident, fool."

The form holding the gun on them chuckled. "I wouldn't be too sure about that, Mrs. Bee." He slowly lifted the light until it skimmed over his face, showing them his identity at last.

Flo sucked in a gasp. "Wilcox Brandt? Why?"

"Because he killed, David Potts," TC said as if all the pieces were finally coming together for her. "The only question is why."

TC wasn't the only one for whom the mystery was finally gelling. Flo suddenly understood. "Because you weren't a good enough scientist to fill Audrey Macintosh's shoes, were you, Will? You knew you were one failed experiment away from getting fired. And you couldn't live with that, could you? So you went to Pott's house to steal their genetically altered rooster, didn't you? Unfortunately, David Potts caught you in the act, so you had to kill him."

Brandt's face was again lost in shadow, but his voice held a note of triumph. "Great story, ladies. Unfortunately, you'll never get a chance to tell it."

The gun lifted, the bright, white glow of the flashlight lifting with it and spilling death-dealing illumination over the three of them.

"Duck!" TC screamed, flinging the only thing she had in her hand, right at him. Her phone hit Brandt's head and bounced harmlessly off.

Brandt's arm jerked up and the gun went off, sending the bullet whizzing right at Tricia Colombo.

There was a scream, then a shout, and the lights came on as TC hit the ground beside Flo and skidded sideways at a pretty good clip, smacking into the wall.

Flo blinked at Agnes, who'd somehow managed to get around her and was standing where TC had been.

"Police! Drop the gun and put your hands up," Detective Peters yelled.

Brandt lifted his hands, the gun still clutched in one of them.

"I said, drop it!" Peters growled out, his entire form rigid with rage and probably a little fear. Flo didn't miss the way he kept glancing toward TC.

Brandt finally complied, slowly bending down and setting the gun on the floor.

"Cover him," Peters yelled to Officer Meldick as he ran toward TC.

He shoved his gun into his belt and knelt down, his handsome face white with terror as he touched her face. "Tricia? What has he done to you?" He ran his hands over her arms and checked her shoulders for bullet holes.

Flo didn't see any blood.

Finally, TC groaned, her eyes fluttering open. "I'm fine."

Peters helped her sit up and she glowered at Agnes. "You didn't have to shove me so hard, Agnes."

Agnes flushed with embarrassment. She rarely knew her own strength. "Sorry."

TC's lips trembled and she finally gave in to a smile. "But thanks for saving my life, girlfriend."

Agnes beamed happily.

Peters helped her stand and stared at her for a beat before tugging her into his arms for a long hug.

TC's eyes went wide over his shoulder and Flo chuckled, immediately regretting it as the knives in her ribs started to dance the jig. "Um, I think I need to have my ribs looked at," she told Agnes.

"I'll drive you to the emergency room," Agnes said, grinning.

Flo resisted another chuckle. "I think we're safe with you driving since it's just up a couple of floors."

"Shotgun!" TC called out from where she still stood, Detective Peters hovering protectively.

It was enough to break the tension of the last few moments and send, at least those who could laugh without crying, into hysterical giggles.

CHAPTER TWENTY-THREE

FLO SHIFTED CAREFULLY on the couch, stilling at the first tweak of pain. Since the debacle at the morgue, she'd learned to move more slowly and breathe shallowly until her broken ribs healed. Down by her feet, Rodney shifted too, grumbling softly, and dropped his little head onto her feet with a contented sigh.

A pillow appeared in front of Flo's face and a big hand shoved it none-too-gently behind her.

Flo bit her lip against the slide of agony across her middle as Agnes helped her get more comfortable. "Thanks, hun. I'm good now." She gently pushed her friend's hand away before Agnes could *help* her into a full body cast.

"Ce's bringing you lunch from *Gioppino's* and Cook brought pie while you were napping."

Flo barely kept from wincing. The last thing she wanted was to eat. "That's nice of them."

"Cook said there was something special about the pie." Agnes frowned. "She told me to be sure and have a piece."

Flo found herself smiling. "Oh good! She was going to bake a sugar-free pie that you could eat, in reasonable amounts, on your new diet plan."

Agnes's eyes lit with pleasure.

A knock on the door preceded a deep male voice. "Mrs. Bee? Can we come in?"

Flo looked at Agnes. "We?" she whispered.

"Come on in," Agnes bellowed.

To Flo's surprise and pleasure, Detective Peters came down the hall and into Flo's living room with his hand firmly clutched in TC's. Their friend had a pretty blush on her face and a happy bounce in her step.

The lovebirds were back together.

Flo was so happy she almost didn't mind the way they'd gotten there. TC had confided to her just that morning that the handsome detective was really shaken by her near miss with that bullet. He'd confessed he'd missed her more than he'd expected, and wanted to discuss their relationship sooner, rather than later.

TC had been happy but wary. She'd told Flo her experience was that, whenever a man wanted to talk about a relationship, there was a good chance the outcome wouldn't be the desired one.

Flo was glad TC had been wrong.

TC dropped into the chair closest to Flo and reached for her hand, squeezing it as she gave Flo an assessing look. "How are you feeling? You still look pale."

"I'm getting a little better every day, hun. That's all I can ask."

TC nodded, glancing towards Peters.

He seemed to take that as his cue. "I—we—wanted to fill you in on the Potts case."

Flo nodded, forgetting her ribs as curiosity replaced pain. "I've been wondering what's going on. Agnes won't tell me." She threw her friend a glare.

Agnes gave her a mulish look, crossing her arms over her chest. "Doc Bombast told me to keep you quiet and calm."

Flo shook her head. Dr. Bombast was a very nice man who came into Silver Hills every week to offer medical aid on minor injuries and illness for the residents. He'd taken it upon himself to keep an eye on Flo after she'd returned home from the hospital.

Flo had always liked the man. Until right at that moment.

Seeing the look on her face, TC patted her arm. "He's just doing his job, Flo. He cares about you. We all do."

She sighed. "I know. I'm just cranky."

Agnes snorted. "I'm going to go make Miss Cranky Pants some tea. Anybody else want something?"

Peters nodded. "Coffee, please. If it wouldn't be too much trouble."

Agnes nodded and headed toward the kitchen. As she passed by the end of the couch, Rodney gave a little growl just to remind her where she stood in his estimation.

"Stuff it, dog," Agnes murmured without even slowing.

Flo motioned toward the recliner facing the couch. "Sit, Detective. Tell me what's been happening."

"Vlad's way down in the polls," TC said with a grin.

"Oh, I know that," Flo said. "I've had nothing to do for a week except lie here and read or watch television. Every time I try to stand up Agnes descends on me like the black plague. Between you and me, I'm in more danger from her than I am from walking across the room to catch a few rays of sun on my face."

"I heard that!" Agnes called out from the kitchen.

Flo flipped her hand dismissively. "Anyway, I'm happy to see the vamp wasn't able to bespell the entire city."

Peters lowered himself into the recliner and shook his head. "No bespelling. Everyone I've talked to hates him. That's no surprise. What does confound me though, is the fact that Newsome actually thought he'd have a chance."

"Delusion, thy name is vampire," Flo said on a grin.

"I think David Junior will make a great mayor," TC said.

"I agree," her boyfriend said.

"So, tell me about Brandt. Were TC and I right? Did he kill Potts because the poor man discovered him trying to steal their special Rooster?"

"That's the short version, yes." Detective Peters leaned forward, resting his forearms on his knees. He was dressed casually, in a denim button-up shirt with a white tee shirt underneath it. Dark wash jeans covered his long legs and were bunched slightly over scuffed, brown boots.

He looked comfortable, and more relaxed than Flo had seen him in a while.

"It's way above my pay grade. But, from what I can piece together after talking to the scientists, that flavor agent Macintosh had been working on didn't exist. It was apparently just cover for a gene-spicing experiment. She'd been splicing human DNA into a chicken in an attempt to create proteins that would cure Alzheimer's. But they discovered the human gene they spliced into the DNA somehow made the chickens larger."

TC grimaced. "Personally, I wouldn't eat a chicken that had human DNA in it, no matter how good it tasted."

Flo's stomach roiled at the thought. "That's why the chicken was at Pott's house instead of with the other chickens. They couldn't afford to let the secret out until they'd figured out a way to sell it," Flo said.

Peters nodded. "Macintosh claims she never intended to sell the chickens for meat, but Potts was apparently pressuring her to figure out a way to make that happen."

"So, what happened with Potts?" Agnes asked, coming back into the room. She handed the detective a steaming mug and Flo a teacup with a delightful aroma.

"Thanks so much, hun." Flo smiled at her friend.

Peters sipped his and nodded his thanks before answering Agnes's question. "When Potts found Wilcox Brandt snooping around, the two men apparently struggled over the bird and Brandt got the best of Potts. He hit him on the head with the flat side of the ax. When Potts fell over that tree trunk, Brandt got the bright idea of trying to make it look like animal activists killed him in revenge for all the chickens he'd slaughtered." Peters arched a brow at Flo. "That scrap of paper you didn't think I saw you take a picture of...?"

Flo flushed guiltily.

"That was a piece of a flyer the group had been posting all over town, including inside the Chisholm's Chickens building. I don't know if he'd seen them at the house or not, but it was safe for Brandt to assume the group had hit Potts Farms too. He figured they'd make good fall guys for the murder."

"Pretty cagey," Flo said. "Excuse the pun."

TC shook her head at the joke. "He'd apparently overheard people at Chisholms talking about how worried they were about violence from the group. He'd torn the flyer down from in front of Chisholm's and had it in his pocket, so the ruse was simple for him," TC clarified, glancing at Peters for validation of the information. He inclined his head.

Flo nodded. "That explains why Potts wanted to hire me. It seems plausible he might have been worried too. Given Potts's personality, since they'd been camped out at his home, he might have gotten into their faces and created such bad blood he could have been getting threats."

"But if that's the case, he would have just told the police, wouldn't he?" TC said, frowning. "I mean, he would have known where the threats came from. He wouldn't have needed Flo to find the person sending them."

"Theoretically," Peters agreed. "But with everything going on at Potts Farms, he probably wouldn't have wanted the police around. And if Flo could catch them off guard and get them to admit the threats, Potts would have had the ammo he needed to have them run off his property and maybe even out of town."

"Why didn't Brandt take the chicken after he killed Potts?" Agnes asked reasonably.

Peters laughed. "He couldn't catch it. He claims the thing's freakishly fast."

Agnes and Flo shared a look. "Among other things," Agnes murmured.

"What about Nanna?" Flo asked. "Was she part of all this?"

"There's nothing to suggest she was," he responded. "Dave Potts kept her pretty isolated from the business," Peters said.

"Though, we think the reason he called you was because of her. She knew you and had heard that you were doing some investigating these days. She believes she mentioned you to her husband once or twice."

"And the boys?"

"They're just as they appear. They wanted nothing to do with Potts Farms either. Everyone I spoke to who knows them says they never have."

"Were Macintosh and Potts having an affair as Nanna suspected?" It didn't really matter anymore, but Flo was curious.

"Macintosh denies it. But I get the feeling she's not being completely honest." He raised his eyebrows. "On a non-related but surprising development, Audrey Macintosh has agreed to return to Chisholm's. She's demanding a new contract and will sell them her Alzheimer's findings outright for a pretty sizeable sum."

"Good for her." Flo said. "Though I sense a rocky path ahead. She's definitely willing to stretch scientific boundaries when she puts her agile mind to something."

Peters nodded his agreement.

Flo thought about the surprising revelation for a moment. Then her mind turned to a question that had been bothering her since she'd had time to reflect on it. "How did Brandt know we were in the morgue that day?" As soon as she voiced the question, she knew. "He followed Roger and me from the diner."

"Very likely," Peters said. "He'd been following you around for a while. He was a worker on David Potts's campaign. Apparently, Nanna addressed the workers after Potts was killed and told them she was planning on hiring you to look into the murder. Brandt panicked. He'd been counting on the police just looking at the nice little scene he'd created and coming to the expected conclusion. But he figured an investigator might be more competent." Peters looked so disgusted by this line of reasoning, Flo felt inclined to make him feel better.

"He obviously doesn't know you, or Detective Nightshade for that matter. You'd never let yourselves fall for such an obvious ploy." Of course, it was unfortunate for the killer that Meanie Meldick hadn't been in charge. He might have been fooled. But Flo wisely refrained from mentioning that to Peters.

"I appreciate your support, Mrs. Bee. However, since Mr. Brandt isn't the sharpest beak in the chicken yard, I choose not to take offense at his opinion."

Flo grinned. "I see what you did there."

Peters shook his head but his lips twitched on a barely suppressed smile.

"Anyway, Brandt decided at that point he'd better keep an eye on you."

"And when we went to the morgue, he figured that was a good place to make sure we didn't learn anything else," Flo said, shuddering.

"He used to work in that lab. He knew the layout and the timetable of the place. He knew just the thing to tell the young lab tech to get Celia's friend, Andy, to run back to the lab, leaving you alone there."

"Little did he know he was leaving us in greater danger by drawing Andy away."

"What do you mean?" Peters asked.

TC looked at Agnes. "He left us alone in a room filled with cutting tools, refrigerated drawers, and Agnes."

Peters barked out a laugh.

Flo couldn't keep from laughing herself, though a sharp stab of pain cut her laughter short.

Agnes glared at TC. "Har, Tricia Colombo. I believe I saved your boohind in the end, though didn't I?"

"Yes you did, and I'll be forever grateful for that." TC's smile turned warm.

"I will too," Peters said, favoring TC with a look that heated the room a few degrees.

Clearing her throat, Flo performed a discreet change of subject. "So what did Brandt tell the lab tech on the phone?"

"He pretended to be a technician from Methodist Hospital in Indianapolis, calling to tell them one of their patients from Silver City had died of a really deadly strain of bird flu and he had reason to suspect one of their bodies might be carrying the virus too."

"Good heavens," Flo breathed.

"Yeah. He's a nasty piece of work."

"He followed us everywhere?" Agnes asked, frowning.

Peters nodded.

"I guess that's why he was in the lane next to us at the *Bounce and Bowl*?"

The detective's eyebrows lifted quizzically. "The Bounce and Bowl?"

"The place where I got my first strike," Agnes said on a grin.

"He was in the next alley and Agnes accidentally clipped him in the ankle with her ball," TC explained.

The detective frowned. "How is that even possible?"

"Don't ask," TC wisely counseled.

Flo barely heard their banter. Detective Peters's words had jarred a realization loose in her brain, inspired by the contented snoring at the other end of the couch. She stared at her dog for a long moment, her emotions raw.

"Mrs. Bee?"

"Flo? What's wrong?"

"Flo, are you in a coma? Snap out of it." Agnes smacked her gently on the arm and jarred her out of her daze. Flo slowly lifted her gaze to Detective Peters. "He poisoned my dog." Her pulse pounded on the memory of a hostile gaze, unexplained and unexpected, as she passed the young man holding the door for her at the emergency clinic that first night.

It had been Wilcox Brandt.

Peters frowned. He'd clearly not wanted her to realize the connection. "I'm afraid so. The moment he heard your name he set out to find you. And I'm afraid Rodney was just a handy tool to try to distract you from the investigation." Peters gave Flo a reproving look. "That list of employees it took you so long to show me..."

Flo flushed. "Sorry, I forgot about it. There was so much going on."

He nodded. "You wouldn't have recognized the name, but Brandt's girlfriend was on it. She works at the clinic. He was there that night to make sure the clump of chicken fat he'd fed to Rodney earlier had done its job."

Flo shivered. The man was a cold-blooded killer and he'd had access to her dog.

She blinked. "How'd he get into my apartment? And, more importantly, how'd he get close enough to Rodney to poison him?"

TC and Peters shared a look. Finally, TC said, "Um, I'm afraid the housekeeper left the door unlocked again."

Flo thought of the woman with the sheets she'd seen in the lobby that night. She pursed her lips, anger spinning through her. The woman's carelessness had nearly killed her dog. "I'm speaking to Richard about that. If he can't find a crew that's more responsible, I'm going to start doing my own dusting and laundry."

TC nodded. "I've already talked to him. We're having a meeting about it later today."

"Good." Flo took a deep breath and sipped her cooling tea. After a moment she felt better.

"Do you want some pie?" Agnes asked.

Flo looked up into her friend's face for the first time since she'd come back into the room. She blinked, a grin finding her face. "Was the cherry pie good?"

Agnes frowned. "How do you know I tasted it?"

TC chuckled happily. "Because you're wearing it on the entire bottom half of your face."

Agnes quickly swiped a big hand over the glossy red mess around her mouth. Her hand came away painted in red. She looked at it, shrugged, and then licked it clean. "It was—is—delicious. I can't even tell it's sugar-free."

TC's eyes went wide. "Sugar-free cherry pie? And it's good?"

Even Peters perked up. "Cherry's my favorite."

Agnes was already heading for the kitchen. I'll make more coffee. And I saw some vanilla ice cream in the freezer.

Flo barely refrained from asking her friend what she was doing snooping in the freezer. She didn't need to ask. She already knew. "The ice cream isn't sugar-free, Agnes," she called out.

"It's okay. I won't have a lot."

Flo looked at TC and shook her head. TC grinned. "Maybe Cook can make sugar free ice cream that doesn't taste like butt too."

"You know, hun. I believe she probably could."

THE END

DID YOU ENJOY FLO AND Agnes's story? If so, you might want to check out the next book in the *Silver Hills Cozy Mysteries* series.

Please enjoy Chapter One of **Love Hertz**:

COME TO SILVER HILLS. Where making friends can prove deadly and creating enemies might be easier than you think.

Emotions are aflutter at Silver Hills as a new heartthrob moves into the residence. Will all that fluttering still a single heart? And if love dies, will Flo's very own *amour* find itself in the crosshairs of the estimable Detective Brent Peters?

Agnes and Hertz are on the outs. Secrets tear the tender fabric of a pulsing heart. What do the secrets have to do with murder?

Affairs of *le cœur* aside, will Agnes break the clothing store shopping for a party dress? What will break during a rousing class of Zumba? And will Flo be able to soldier through her dance injuries to follow a chubby cherub to a killer?

So many questions. So much hopping, tapping and fluttering. And still a murder to solve.

What will Flo and Co. do?

They'll do what they always do, of course. Hearts out and chins up, they're goin' in!

CHAPTER ONE

"COME ON, FLO. I'VE seen ants that can lift more than that."

Flo glared at her friend, her muscles quivering under the strain of the metal weights. "I'm gonna lift these right up to your head if you don't stop razzing me," she told Agnes.

"I'm not razzing. I'm motivating."

Climbing a virtual mountain in a digital headwind on a nearby stationary bike, Celia Angonetti snorted. "Apparently, Agnes went to the Marine Drill Sargent school of motivation."

Flo shook her head. "I'm not a fan of that motivational style, Agnes," she told her friend. "If you don't stop, I'm going to show you some motivation with one of these weights."

Agnes rolled her gray eyes. "Fine. Then let me try a different style." She curved her lips into a fake smile. "I'm definitely seeing some improvement, Flo. I think your arms are looking less baby-bird-like and more like stalks of anemic celery."

With a groan, Flo handed the weights to Agnes, pushing herself into a sitting position on the bench. She shoved fingers into her newly styled, light-brown bouff, trying to fluff it up again. "I can't tell you how motivated that makes me feel," she told Agnes. "Thanks so much."

"You're welcome." Agnes placed the seven-pound weights back into the holder. "I was going to ask you to spot me while I lift, but you'd probably drop the weights on my head with those spindly girl arms."

Growling under her breath, Flo swiped a towel over her glistening face. "What's got your bloomers in a twist this morning, Agnes? Did you accidentally eat a raisin in your oatmeal?"

She grimaced. "Not a chance. I can smell those wrinkly disasters a mile away."

When a frown continued to blossom on her friend's wide face, Flo tried again. "What is it?"

Agnes glanced at Celia, who'd conquered the peak of the virtual mountain and was happily spinning downward, her slender form bathed in sweat and a smile on her face.

Agnes led Flo away from their friend. "It's Hertz. He's thinking about moving out of Silver Hills."

Hertz was Agnes' new boyfriend. The two of them had become almost inseparable of late. To the point where Flo kind of missed spending time with her friend. It didn't help that things had been really slow in her private investigation business. Nobody'd tried to hire her for a couple of months.

Flo was getting antsy. "Why? I thought he loved it here."

"He does." Agnes skimmed the graying brown strands of her chin-length pageboy behind her ears. She grabbed a twenty-pound weight from the stand and proceeded to work a muscular right arm as she spoke to Flo. "I think it's a money thing, but I can't get him to talk to me about it."

"Oh, dear," Flo said. "I'm so sorry, Agnes. I'd be sad to see him go. But just because he moves out of Silver Hills doesn't mean you can't still see each other."

"I know. But it just won't be the same." She switched the weight to her other hand and repeated the reps on that arm.

"Do you want me to talk to Richard?"

Richard Attles was the day manager at Silver Hills. He was also Roger Attles' son and, since Roger and Flo were a bit of an item themselves, she had some influence over Richard. "Maybe there's a studio apartment coming available. "The studios were very popular and there were rarely vacancies for one. But they did have one they used for display purposes. "Maybe he could move into a display if he agreed to let the managers show it when they had an interested party."

Agnes settled the weight back into the holder, her frown softening. "That's not a bad idea. He can save a thousand a month if he switches to a studio." Her brow furrowed again. "But I know he loves living in his dad's old place. He might not want to move."

Hertz had lost his father a few months earlier, and he'd kept his dad's apartment. Flo thought it was mostly because he wanted to stay close to Agnes. The two of them had hit it off immediately, bonding over their love of food, movies, and cats. "We can give it a try. I'll talk to Roger about it before we go to Richard. Roger and Hertz have gotten pretty close. He might have some idea what's going on there."

Agnes nodded, still looking worried. "Thanks, Flo."

"Of course, hun." Flo gave her a smile. "But you don't look any happier."

Agnes grabbed the towel she'd draped around the back of her neck and dried her face with it. "I need to get going. Hertz and I are going to a movie tonight."

Celia joined them, her own towel clutched in one hand and her pretty face aglow from her efforts. "Are you going to see that *Clue* remake? I'm trying to get Mass to go with me to see it, but he says trying to figure out who offed someone was too much like his day job to be fun."

Massimo Angonetti was Celia's sort-of-estranged gangster husband. They were still married but lived separately. Most likely to give Celia plausible deniability with Mass' career. He'd technically never gotten busted by PoPo for doing anything illegal, but his partial fingerprints were probably all over a hundred different crime scenes.

"No," Agnes frowned. "We're going to see a science fiction film." Her lips curled slightly. He knows I hate those," she murmured.

Watching her, Flo wondered what was really bothering her friend. "Why don't you tell him you aren't interested in going to that movie then?"

Agnes shrugged. "I'll see you guys later."

Watching Agnes' six-foot-tall form shuffle out of the gym, worry settled into Flo's belly with the weight of an overbaked scone.

"Trouble in paradise?" Ce asked, slipping her arm through Flo's.

"Could be," Flo agreed. "I sure hope not, though. Agnes has been so happy since Hertz moved into Silver Hills."

"She won't talk about it?" Ce grabbed her water bottle and they headed toward the door.

"Not yet. But I'm not done pestering her. If there's something I can do to help them I want to do it."

Holding the door, Ce nodded. "I'll offer her two free dinners to *Gioppino's* for a Saturday night. That's the night the new Jazz quartet plays. A little candlelight and romantic music might help."

Flo squeezed Ce's arm against her side. "You're the best, Ce. That might be just the ticket."

"There you are, doll."

Flo turned at the sound of Roger Attles' voice. She smiled when she saw him, shoving self-consciously at her bouff where it had been mashed against the weight bench. "Hey, Roger."

Flo slid her smile toward the man he was walking with. "Hello."

"Well hello, beautiful." The man had steel-gray hair, close-cropped and dense on his well-shaped head, and quicksilver gray eyes to match. His startling gaze was enhanced by a thick fringe of black lashes and strong eyebrows that slashed dramatically across his tanned face.

He was almost as tall as Roger but built like an athlete, where Roger was built like a lawyer.

"Doll, this is Nicholai Pearce. He just moved into Silver Hills."

The other man nodded. "I've been staying at a motel just outside of town for a couple of months while I looked for the perfect place to live," he clarified. "I'm thrilled I was able to grab an apartment here at Silver Hills. It's not an easy place to get into."

"It is very popular," she agreed smiling. It's so nice to meet you, Nicholai," Flo shook his hand.

He bent over her hand and placed a kiss on the back, drawing a frown from Roger. "Call me Nic, please. And the pleasure is all mine, Flo."

He said her name like a caress, making her cheeks heat.

"If you'll excuse me. I have a thing..."

Flo turned in surprise to watch Celia walk away, her strides brisk. That was strange. Celia was usually one of the first to greet new residents. Flo flushed with embarrassment. "I'm sorry, she...um...had a thing. How are you enjoying Silver Hills so far?" Flo asked Nic, noting the way his dark brows had lowered as he watched Ce leave.

"It's just great, Flo. The people have been so kind." He tore his gaze from Celia's retreat and pounded Roger on the back, grinning widely. "Old Roger here has already invited me to poker night. Everyone's been so welcoming, I feel as if I've lived here all my life."

"You obviously haven't met the vampires yet, then," Flo joked.

When Nic frowned in confusion, she glanced at Roger. "You haven't warned him about Vlad and Morty?"

"I didn't want to scare him away, doll. It's only his second day in the residence."

Flo laughed. "Well, make sure you fill him in." She grinned. "How does your wife enjoy it so far? I'd love to meet her."

Nic looked at the gold band on his finger, frowning. "I'm afraid I lost her last year."

He looked so miserable, Flo wanted to kick herself. "Oh, I'm so sorry."

"Not your fault. You didn't know. It's actually one of the reasons I moved here. I got tired of bumbling around in that big house all by myself. I thought it would be good for me to be around more people."

"Well, you've definitely come to the right place then," Flo laughed. "You just got yourself a couple hundred nosy neighbors."

"I'm looking forward to getting to know my neighbors better," Nic said, his voice warm. "Much better."

She realized with a start that he was flirting with her. Flo stood in stunned silence for a long moment, unsure how to respond. Finally, Roger cleared his throat. "Well, we're going to be late for poker." He reached over and took Flo's hand, kissing her on the cheek in a maneuver Flo couldn't help reading as marking his territory. "I'll see you later, doll."

"It was nice meeting you," she said awkwardly to Nic. Then she hurried toward the stairs that led down to her apartment on the second floor. Anxious to put some space between herself and their new neighbor. Something about the man bothered her. It wasn't just that he was an outrageous flirt. Although she'd always hated that in a man. It was that he'd flirted with her right in front of Roger when it seemed pretty clear that they were an item.

Celia's response to Nicholai Pearce had been strange. And really out of character for her friend, who was usually very welcoming.

Flo decided she needed to find Ce and ask her about her reaction to the new resident.

"Mrs. Bee?"

She jolted to a stop at the familiar voice, turning to find Hertz Thomson striding quickly in her direction. "Can I speak with you for a moment?"

Flo frowned, not wanting to get in the middle of Agnes' and Hertz's relationship issues. "Of course." She smiled as he stopped in front of her, saying a silent prayer that he just wanted to ask her about something non-relationship related.

Unfortunately, luck was not Flo's lady at the moment.

"I'm glad I caught you," Hertz said, his gaze skimming the area as if looking for someone. "I wanted to talk to you about Agnes..."

Flo held up a hand. "Let me stop you right there, Mr. Thomson..."

"Hertz, please."

"If you'll call me Flo."

He smiled. "Flo. I'm sorry to bother you. I promise I'm not trying to put you in the middle. It's just..." His face folded into a frown, frustration oozing off him. "You know Agnes better than almost anyone."

"I'd like to think I do," she told him. "But she doesn't discuss her relationships with me."

He nodded. "I get that. This is a more...general...question." He twined his hands together, skimming another glance around the floor.

"Out with it, Hertz," Flo said, her tone firm but not unkind. She did feel for him. Romance was hard under the best circumstances, and dealing with a woman who'd spent most of her life alone couldn't be a picnic in the park.

"I need some advice on how to get Agnes to understand why I'm moving."

Flo was caught off guard and said the first thing that popped into her mind. "She thinks you're dumping her."

He expelled air. "I knew it."

"Are you saying that you're not dumping her? Because, if you are, then you should be talking to her, not me."

He shook his head. "I wish it was that simple."

Flo raised her brows, her temper flaring.

He seemed to understand his mistake right away. "That didn't come out the way I meant it. What I'm trying to say is..." He sighed. "I really care for Agnes..."

Flo could hear the "but" coming a mile away. She lifted a hand to stop him. "Nope. I'm not interested in your excuses, Mr. Thomson. Agnes is a wonderful woman. You're lucky that she cares for you. If you intend to break her heart, my advice is to do it quickly and get out of her life so she can pick up the pieces." Flo turned away, her footsteps heavy on the carpet.

She pressed her lips together to keep from giving the younger man what for and hurried to her apartment, hoping to lock herself inside before her mouth opened and spewed all the ugliness her mind was thinking about him.

Flo embraced her anger as she pushed inside, sidestepping her eager, bouncing dachshund as she closed the door firmly behind her.

Rodney needed to go outside and potty, but she wanted to make sure Hertz Thomson had vacated the hallway before she went back out there. Flo didn't trust herself not to smack the man upside the head if she saw him again.

VISIT THE SILVER HILLS book page on Sam's website for more information and purchase links!
https://samcheever.com/books/#SilverHills

WHAT'S NEXT?

READ MORE OF SAM'S Work: Did you enjoy the book? If you'd like to read more books like this from Sam Cheever, check out her other bestselling books:

Silver Hills Cozy Mysteries: https://samcheever.com/books/#SilverHills

Country Cousin Mysteries: https://samcheever.com/books/#Country

Gainfully Employed Mysteries: https://samcheever.com/books/#gainfully

Grave Theatrics Mysteries: https://samcheever.com/books/#grave

Enchanting Inquiries Mysteries: https://samcheever.com/books/#enchanting

Provide Reviews: If you enjoy the books, please consider showing support for Sam by leaving reviews so that other readers will know what to expect from a Sam Cheever book. Book reviews help readers as well as authors!

Connect: If you'd like to stay up to date on Sam's News, Releases and Appearances, consider liking her Facebook Page, following her on Twitter, and signing up for her Newsletter:

Newsletter: https://samcheever.com/newsletter/

Website: https://www.SamCheever.com

Blog: https://samcheever.com/blog/

Facebook: https://www.facebook.com/SamCheever-Author

Bookbub: https://www.bookbub.com/authors/sam-cheever

Goodreads: https://www.goodreads.com/author/show/1812031.Sam_Cheever

ABOUT THE AUTHOR

USA TODAY AND WALL Street Journal Bestselling Author Sam Cheever writes mystery and suspense, creating stories that draw you in and keep you eagerly turning pages. Known for writing great characters, snappy dialogue, and unique and exhilarating stories, Sam is the award-winning author of 100+ books.

To learn more about Sam and her work, visit her at one of her online hotspots:

Website[1] | Facebook[2] | Goodreads[3] | Blog[4]

1. http://www.samcheever.com/

2. https://www.facebook.com/pages/Sam-Cheever-Author/102117321982

3. http://www.goodreads.com/author/show/1812031.Sam_Cheever

4. http://samcheever.com/blog

www.ingramcontent.com/pod-product-compliance
Lightning Source LLC
Chambersburg PA
CBHW060543260626
47161CB00003B/1035